WANTED: ONE WEDDING DRESS

**Three brides in search
of the perfect dress—
and the perfect husband!**

Welcome to this fabulous new trilogy by talented
Presents™ author Sharon Kendrick. On a bride's
special day, there's nothing more important to
her than a beautiful wedding dress—apart from
the perfect bridegroom! Meet three women who
are about to find both....

This month, meet wedding-dress designer
Holly Lovelace in **One Bridegroom Required!**
Actually, it's Holly's mother who has designed
and made the spectacular dress that Holly wears
for her wedding!

In March, that very same dress is worn by
Amber for her big day in **One Wedding
Required!** And in **One Husband Required!** in
April, the dress gets a third and final airing when
Amber's sister, Ursula, walks up the aisle in it,
too!

Read on and share the excitement as Holly,
Amber and Ursula meet and marry their
bridegrooms!

Dear Reader,

Planning a wedding is like writing your first book—you should stick with what you know! My husband and I were flat broke when we got married, and the only way to guarantee a show-stopping dress was to have it made for me (refusing to accept that my curvy shape looked nothing like the supermodel on the front of the pattern!). So I bought slippery satin and filmy organza and the dress was made and...

And I looked like a whale!

Two weeks before the ceremony, I had to rush out to buy a replacement dress. Luckily I found one—but I ended up with two wedding dresses and a lot of extra expense!

With weddings, it's best to play safe....

At least until after the service is over!

Sharon Kendrick

Sharon Kendrick

One Bridegroom Required!

WANTED: ONE
WEDDING DRESS

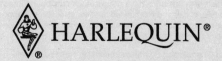

HARLEQUIN®

TORONTO • NEW YORK • LONDON
AMSTERDAM • PARIS • SYDNEY • HAMBURG
STOCKHOLM • ATHENS • TOKYO • MILAN • MADRID
PRAGUE • WARSAW • BUDAPEST • AUCKLAND

With thanks to the vivacious, flame-haired Jill Robinson and her velvet-voiced colleagues at Hamptons International, Winchester, England.

ISBN 0-373-12011-7

ONE BRIDEGROOM REQUIRED!

First North American Publication 1999.

Printed in U.S.A.

PROLOGUE

THE wedding dress gleamed indistinctly through its heavy shrouding of plastic.

It was an exquisite gown—simple and striking and fashioned with care from ivory silk-satin. Organza whispered softly beneath the skirt and the matching veil was made of gossamer-fine tulle.

At a little over twenty years old, it was ageless and timeless, a future heirloom—to be passed down from bride to bride, each woman adapting it and making it uniquely hers.

But for now it remained locked in a wardrobe, hidden and protected and unworn.

And waiting....

CHAPTER ONE

LUKE GOODWIN stood in front of the big, Georgian window and gave a sigh of satisfaction which not even the bleak November day could dispel. He stared at the unfamiliar landscape before him. It was a loveless time of year in England, once the last of the leaves had fallen.

The sky was as grey as slush and the clouds had an ominous bulge which spoke of heavy rains to come. It was as unlike the golden and blue African skies he had left behind as it was possible to be.

Yet the green chequerboard of fields which stretched as far as his eye could see was now his. As was this graceful old house with enough bedrooms to sleep a football team. His hard mouth softened into a smile as he tried to take it all in, but it was hard to believe that this, all this beauty, now belonged to him.

Oh, a different type of beauty from the one he was used to, that was for sure. His beauty had been searing heat and blazing cerulean skies. The scent of lemons and the puff of fragrant smoke wafting from the barbecue. There had been bare rooms where giant fans cast their flickering circles across bleached ceilings—so different from the elegant Georgian drawing room in which he now stood.

He had been here only eight hours and yet felt he knew the house as intimately as any lover. He had arrived in the middle of the night, but had walked the echoing floors in silence, examining each room and reac-quainting himself with each chair, each moulding. Running his long fingers along their pure, clean surfaces with the awe of a mother studying her newborn.

His heart sang with possession—not for the house's worth, but for its link with the past, and the future. Like a rudderless boat, Luke had finally found the mooring of his dreams.

He let his eyes grow accustomed to the view. Through an arched yew hedge was a clutch of thatched cottages, a pub, a few tasteful and essential shops—as well as the added bonus of a village green with accompanying duck pond. England at its most picture-perfect. His senses were stretched with fatigue, and the soft beauty of his childhood home had never seemed quite so poignant.

Next month Caroline would arrive from Africa, in time for Christmas. Caroline who, despite her associa-tions with that country, was the epitome of an English rose. Caroline with her soft, understated beauty and her unflappability and her resourcefulness. Not his usual kind of woman at all...

Somehow, God only knew how, she had arranged for a woman to come and clean the house for him. She hadn't let the matter of a few thousand miles affect her organisational skills!

He guessed it was yet another indication of how much his tastes had matured. Luke's wild and rollicking ad-venturing days were over, and he was ready to take on all the responsibilities which his inheritance had brought. Sometimes your life changed and there wasn't a damned thing you could do about it.

Luke smiled the contented smile of a man who had found what he was looking for.

Life, he decided, was just like a giant jigsaw puzzle, and the last piece had just slotted effortlessly into place.

Holly clicked off the ignition key just before the engine cut out of its own accord in the middle of the narrow village street. Number ninety-nine on her list of things to do, she thought with dark humour—change her car.

If only she didn't love it so much! An ancient old Beetle which she had lovingly painted herself, because that was the kind of thing that students did. It was just that she wasn't a student any more...

She slowly got out of the car and stood on the pavement, staring up at the empty building with eyes which half refused to believe that this shop was now *hers*.

Lovelace Brides. The place where every bride-to-be would want to buy the wedding outfit of her wildest and most wonderful dreams. Where she, Holly Lovelace, intended to transform each woman who set foot over that threshold into the most amazing bride imaginable!

Holly shivered. She should have worn her thermals. The November air had a really hungry bite to it and the gauzy shirt she was wearing would be better suited to a summer's day.

Still, now was the time to open up the shop, and then just haul her stuff inside and unpack the basics—like vests and tea bags! She could risk moving the car later.

She was just fishing around in her shoulder bag for the great clump of keys which seemed to have got lost among all the clutter at the bottom, when she heard the sound of footsteps approaching.

Holly looked up sharply and her hair tumbled in cop-per-curled disarray all over her shoulders. She felt her mouth fall open in slow motion as she focussed on the man walking towards her, then blinked, as if her eyes were playing tricks on her. She blinked again. No, they weren't. Holly stared, then swallowed.

He was quite the most gorgeous man she had ever seen, and yet somehow he looked kind of *wrong* walking down the sleepy village street. Holly frowned. It wasn't just that he was tall, or tanned, or lean where it counted—though he was all of these, and more. Or that his broad shoulders and rugged frame spoke of a man you didn't mess with. Holly looked a little closer. His hair was dark—dark as muscovado sugar—and the ends were tipped with gold.

He wore jeans, but proper, workmanlike jeans—faded by constant use and hard work, not from stone-washing in a factory. And they weren't sprayed on so tightly that any movement looked an impossibility—with legs like *his* they wouldn't need to be.

With his thick cream sweater and battered sheepskin jacket, he looked vital and vibrant—like a Technicolor image superimposed on an old black-and-white film. More real than real. He made the drizzly grey of the day seem even more insignificant and Holly found that she couldn't drag her eyes away from him.

He came to a halt right in front of her, jeaned legs astride, returning her scrutiny with a mocking stare of his own.

Now she could see that his eyes were blue—bluer than the sea, even bluer than a summer's sky. A dreamer's eyes. An adventurer's eyes.

Holly felt that if she didn't speak she would do something unforgivable—like reach her hand out and touch the hard, tanned curve of his jaw. Just for the hell of it.

'Hello,' she smiled, thinking that if all the men in Woodhampton looked like this, then she was going to be very happy working here!

He stared back, at dark copper curls and white skin and green eyes, the colour of jealousy. For Luke it was like being stun-gunned—that was the only thing he could think of right then. Or hit, maybe. A physical blow might explain the sudden unbearable throbbing of his blood, the heated dilation of the veins in his face. He could feel his mouth roughen and dry and the beginning of an insistent ache in a certain part of his anatomy which filled him with sudden self-loathing.

The woman was a complete stranger—so how in hell had unwanted desire incapacitated him so completely and so mercilessly and so bloody *suddenly*?

Holly had to concentrate very hard to stop her knees from buckling, since her long legs seemed to have nothing to do with her all of a sudden. And why on earth was he *staring* at her like that?

'Hello,' she said again, only more coolly this time, because it wasn't very flattering to be ignored. 'Have we met before?'

His expression didn't change, but his voice was impatient. 'Don't play games. You know damned well we haven't.' He treated her to a parody of a smile. 'Or I think we would have remembered. Don't you?'

His voice was deep and dark, his accent impossible to define, and yet his words were mocking. Made her question into a meaningless little platitude. Yet he was right. She *would* have remembered. This was a man you would never forget. He would stamp his presence indelibly on your heart and mind and eyes.

Holly gave him a sideways look. 'Perhaps I would.' She shrugged quietly. 'I've certainly had better greetings in my life.'

'Oh, I bet you have, sweetheart,' he agreed softly, and managed to make the words sound like an insult. 'I *bet* you have.'

Suddenly Holly wished she were wearing some neat little boxy suit and a pair of tights, with shoes you could see your face in, instead of a faded pair of denims and a too-thin shirt. Maybe then he'd wipe that hungry, mean-looking expression off his face and show her a little respect. Though respect you had to earn, and she wasn't sure she'd care to earn anything from him…

'So what do you want?' she asked, not caring if it sounded abrupt. 'You must want *something*, the way you're staring at me like you've just seen a ghost—unless I have a smudge on my nose, or something?'

Staring at the pure lines of her lips, which were untouched by lipstick, Luke felt fingers of fantasy enmeshing him in their grasp. 'You haven't,' he told her huskily. 'And as to what I want, well, that rather depends—'

'On?'

He bit back the crude, unaccustomed sexual request he was tempted to make and channelled it instead into indignation, clipping out his words like bullets as he pointed to her Beetle. 'On whether that rust bucket of a car happens to belong to you, or not?'

'And if it does?' She tipped her head back and narrowed her eyes, and her hair swung in a copper curtain all the way down her back.

'If it does, then it's the worst piece of parking I've seen in my life!' he drawled.

Holly saw the light of combat sparking in the depth of unforgettable blue eyes and wondered what was causing this definite overreaction. Bad experience? 'Oh, dear. Have you got a thing about women drivers?' she asked him sweetly.

'Not at all. Just bad drivers.' His mouth flattened into a hard line. 'Though most women seem to need a space the size of an airstrip to park.'

Holly almost laughed until she saw that he meant it. She shook her head slowly. 'Heavens!' she murmured. 'I can't believe that anyone would come out with an outdated sexist remark like that, not when we're almost into the millennium—talk about a gross generalisation!'

Luke found himself mesmerised by her eyes. Too green, he thought suddenly. Too wide and too deep. For the first time in his life he understood the expression 'eyes you could drown in'. Tension caused his throat to tighten up. 'Really?' he drawled huskily. 'Not even if it happens to be true? That's usually how generalisations come into being.'

Holly's mouth twitched. Very clever; but not clever enough. She wasn't going to let him get away with that. 'You've done comparative research on male and female parking behaviour, have you?'

'I don't need to, sweetheart. I base my opinions on my own experience.'

'And your experience of women is extensive, no doubt?'

'Pretty much.' His gaze was cool as it flicked over her, and then suddenly not so cool. 'But you still haven't told me whether it's your car, or not?'

He knew damn well it was! Holly held her palms up in supplication. 'Okay, I admit it, Officer,' she told him mockingly, and then dangled the keys from her finger provocatively. 'The car is mine!'

It had been a long time since a woman had made fun of him quite so audaciously. 'Then might I suggest you *move* it?' he suggested softly.

Her eyes narrowed at the unfriendliness in his tone. 'Why the hell should I?'

'Because not only is it an eyesore—it's dangerous!'

It occurred to her briefly that if it had been anyone else talking to her in this way, then she would have asked them to show her a little courtesy. So why let *him* get away with it? Because he looked like her every fantasy come to life? Every other woman's fantasy, come to that.

A voice in her head told her that she was playing with fire, but she didn't listen to it, and afterwards she would cringe when she remembered what she said next. And the way she said it. 'Only if you ask me nicely,' she pouted.

Luke drew in a deep breath of outrage and desire, his mind dizzy with the scent of her, his eyes dazzled by the slim, pale column of her neck, the ringlets which floated down over her ripe, pointed breasts.

She looked like a student, he thought hungrily, with her well-worn denims and that gauzy-looking top, which was much too cold for winter weather and made the tips of her breasts thrust towards him. He forced himself to avert his eyes because he'd known plenty of women like this one. Foxy. Easy. Too easy. Women like this were put on this earth with no purpose other than to tempt.

And he was through with women like that.

He thought of Caroline, and swallowed down his guilt and his lust. 'Just do it, will you?' he told her dismissively. And he walked on without another look or glance—even though he could feel her eyes burning indignantly into his back.

Holly hadn't felt so mad for years, but then she couldn't ever remember being spoken to like that by a man. Not ever. The men she had met at college were 'in touch' with their feminine sides—strong on respect, weak on sex appeal. Not like him.

She stared at his retreating form and winced, wondering how she could have been so cloying and so *obvious*. Pouting at him like the school tease. But then sometimes you found yourself reacting in inexplicable ways to certain people—and she suspected that he was the type of man who provoked strong reactions.

Still. Men were a fact of life—even irascible ones. No, *especially* irascible ones! And she was a businesswoman now—she simply couldn't afford to let herself get uptight just because someone had got out of the wrong side of bed that morning. She watched him push open the door to the general store at the end of the street, telling herself that she was glad to see the back of him.

She unlocked the shop door and stepped over a stack of old mail and circulars. She hadn't been here since the summer, on one of the most beautiful, golden days of the year, when she had taken the lease on, and she found herself wondering what the shop would look like in this cold and meagre November light.

Inside it was so gloomy that Holly could barely see. She clicked on the light switch and then blinked while her eyes accustomed themselves to the glare thrown off by the naked lightbulb, and her heart fell. It obviously hadn't been touched since the day she had signed the lease.

The air wasn't just thick with dust—it was *clogged* with it, and cobwebs were looped from the ceiling like ghostly necklaces, giving the interior of the shop the appearance of an outdated horror movie. It might have been funny if it hadn't been her livelihood at stake.

Holly scowled, then coughed. Dust was the enemy of all fabrics, but it was death to the exquisite fabrics she tended to work with. So. What did she do first? Unpack the car? Make a cup of tea? Or make inroads into the neglect?

She half closed her eyes and tried to imagine just what the place would look like all decorated with big mirrors and fresh paint. Dramatic colours providing a rich foil for the snowy, showy gowns. But it was no good—for once her imagination stubbornly refused to work.

A dark shadow fell over her and Holly turned her head to see the man with the denim-blue eyes standing in the doorway. He stepped into the shop as if he had every right to.

He made the interior feel terribly claustrophobic. Holly found herself distracted by those endless legs, the dizzying width of his shoulders, and she felt a warm, unfamiliar tightening in her belly. He was, she noticed inconsequentially, carrying two cartons of milk, a box of chocolate biscuits and a newspaper. So—whoever he was—he certainly didn't have much in the way of domestic routine!

'Well, hello again,' said Holly, and smiled into the denim-coloured eyes.

'What in hell's name are you doing in *here*?'

'I'm admiring all the dust and cobwebs—what does it look like?'

'That isn't what I meant and you know it!' he growled. 'How did you get in here?'

Holly stared at him as if he'd gone completely mad. 'How do you think I got in? By picking the lock?'

He shrugged his massive shoulders as if to say that nothing would surprise him. 'Tell me.'

'I used my key, of course!'

'Your *key*?'

'Yes,' she defended, wondering if he always glared at people this much. She waved the offending item in front of him. 'My key! See!'

'And how did you get hold of a key?'

'I clutched it between my fingers and thumb, just like everyone else does!'

'Don't be facetious!'

'Well, what do you expect when you come over so heavy? How on earth do you think I got it? It's mine. On loan. I'm renting.'

'*Renting?*'

Her mouth twitched. 'Do you know—you have a terrible habit of repeating everything I say and making it into a question?'

'You're renting the shop?' he persisted in disbelief, as though she hadn't spoken. 'This shop?'

'That's right.'

'Why?'

Holly smiled at his belligerence. 'Well, you've barged in here as if you own the place, asking me questions as though I'm on the witness stand, so I suppose one more won't make any difference. Why do people usually rent a shop? Because they want to sell something, perhaps? Like me—I'm a dress designer.'

He nodded. 'Yes,' he agreed slowly, and an ironic smile touched the corners of his mouth. 'Yes, you look like a dress designer.'

Holly noted the disapproving look on his face and was glad she wasn't opening an escort agency! 'Is that supposed to be a compliment?'

'No.'

'I didn't think so. I fit the stereotype, do I?'

He shrugged. 'I guess you do.' His eyes flickered to the gauzy shirt, where the stark outline of her nipples bore testimony to the cold weather. 'You wear unsuitable clothes. You drive a hand-painted, beaten-up old car—I wasn't for a minute labouring under the illusion that you were a bank clerk!'

'Nothing wrong with bank clerks,' Holly defended staunchly.

'I didn't say there was,' came his soft reply. 'So tell me why you're renting this shop.'

'To sell my designs.'

He frowned as he tried to picture the insubstantial and outrageous garments in which emaciated models sashayed up the catwalk. He tried to imagine Caroline or any other woman he knew wearing one. And the only one who *could* get away with it was the leggy beauty standing in front of him. 'Think there'll be a market for them around here, do you?' he mocked. 'It's a pretty conservative kind of area.'

She ignored the sarcasm. 'I certainly hope so! There's always a market for bridal gowns—'

His dark eyebrows disappeared beneath the tawny hair. '*Bridal* gowns?'

'There you go again,' she murmured. 'Yes. Bridal gowns. You know—the long white frocks that women wear on what is supposed to be the happiest day of their lives.' She waited for him to say something about *his* wedding day, which was what people always *did* say. But he didn't. And Holly was both alarmed and astonished at the great sensation of relief which flooded through her at his lack of reaction. *He isn't married!* she found herself thinking with a feeling which was very close to elation, and then hoped she hadn't given anything away in her expression.

'You design *bridal gowns*?'

'You sound surprised.'

'Maybe that's because I am. You aren't exactly what most people have in mind when they think of wedding dresses.'

'Too young?' she guessed.

'There's that,' he agreed. 'And marriage is traditional...' his eyes glimmered '...which you ain't.'

'I can be. I know how to be.'

Interesting. 'And you'll be living—?'

'In the flat upstairs, of course.' She smiled in response to his frowned reaction to *that*, and wiped a dusty hand down the side of her jeans before extending her hand. 'I guess we'd better introduce ourselves. I'm Holly

Lovelace of Lovelace Brides.' She smiled disarmingly. 'Who are you?'

'Holly *Lovelace*?' He started to laugh.

'That's right.'

'Not your real name, right?'

'Wrong. I've got my birth certificate somewhere, if you'd like to check.'

He looked down at the hand she was still holding out, and shook it, her narrow fingers seeming to get lost within the grasp of his big, rough palm. 'I'm Luke Goodwin,' he said deliberately, and waited.

'Hello, Luke!'

There was another brief pause as he savoured a heady feeling of power. 'You haven't heard of me?'

'You're absolutely right. I haven't.'

'Well, I'm your new landlord.'

Holly was too busy blinking up at him to respond at first. Up this close he was even more divine. He had the kind of mouth that even the most hardened man-hater would have described as irresistible. She was just wondering what it would be like to be kissed by a mouth like that when his words seeped unwillingly into her consciousness.

'But you can't be my landlord!' she protested. Landlords were pallid and wore pinstriped suits, not faded jeans and a golden tan which she suspected might be all over.

He slanted a look at her from between sultry azure eyes. 'Oh? Says who?'

'Says me! You're not the person I signed the lease with!'

'And who did you sign the lease with?'

'I had to meet a man in Winchester—'

'Called?'

'Doug Something-or-Other…' Holly frowned as she recalled the smoothie who had tried plying her with gin and tonics in the middle of the day and sat leering at her thighs. His oily attitude had had a lot to do with the speed with which she had signed the lease. 'I know! Doug Reasdale, that was it.'

'Doug's the letting agent,' he informed her. 'He acted for my uncle.'

'Well, he certainly didn't mention that there was an absentee and highly hostile landlord!' snapped Holly.

'No longer absentee,' he amended thoughtfully. 'And Doug neglected to mention to *me* that he'd just rented out one of my properties to someone who doesn't even look old enough to vote!'

'I'm twenty-six, actually,' she corrected him tightly. She was getting fed up with people thinking she was just a kid. Maybe it was time she started wearing a little make-up, maybe even cut her hair…

'Twenty-six, huh?' He looked at the wild tangle of her curls and her wide-spaced green eyes. Bare lips that excited…invited… Right at that moment she looked like jail bait. 'Well, maybe you should try acting it,' he suggested softly.

Holly smirked. 'Really? That's neat, coming from you! You mean I should follow your shining example of adult behaviour and start throwing my weight around? I thought that dictatorships had gone out of fashion until I met you!'

'But clearly a very ineffective dictatorship in this case,' he observed, trying very hard not to laugh, 'since

I asked you to move your car, but it still seems to be taking up half the road!'

'You didn't *ask* me anything!' she fumed. 'You issued the kind of order that I haven't heard since I was at school!'

'Then you were obviously a very disobedient school-girl,' he murmured, before realising that the conversation was in danger of sliding helplessly into sexual innuendo and that he was in very great danger of responding to it.

Holly had never met a man she found as physically attractive as the one standing in front of her, and maybe his allure was responsible for what she did next. She tried to tell herself that it was purely an instinctive re-action to that suggestive velvet whisper, but, whatever the reason, she found herself slanting her eyes at him like a courtesan. 'Why?' she murmured provocatively, and put her hands on her hips. 'Have you got a thing about schoolgirls?'

Luke froze. When she leaned back like that it was easy to see that she wasn't wearing a bra, that her lush breasts were free and unfettered. He saw the way her lips were parted into a smile and he knew for certain that, if he tried to kiss her right then, she would melt into his arms in the way that so many women had done before. But no more. His mouth hardened.

'I'll tell you what I have a ''thing'' about,' he said carefully. 'And that's people who take on more than they're obviously capable of—'

'Meaning me?'

'Meaning you,' he agreed evenly, as he fought to keep his feelings under control. 'You clearly can't tell your left from your right, judging by your parking—so heaven only knows how you intend to run a thriving business! Or maybe that's why you enjoy flirting with me so outrageously. Maybe you suspect that you're destined to fail? Perhaps you like to have a little something to fall back on, huh? So that if your business goes bust, then the landlord might be lenient with you.'

Holly stared at him, first in horror, then in disbelief. Then with an irresistible desire to giggle. 'My God, you're actually being *serious*, aren't you? Are you really from planet Earth, or have aliens just dropped you here? Or do you honestly think that I'd leap into bed with you if I didn't have enough money to pay the rent?'

Luke knew that he had two choices. If he allowed her to think that he had actually *meant* that outrageous suggestion, then she would seriously underestimate his critical judgement—and Luke didn't like being underestimated by *anyone*. If she underestimated him then she wouldn't respect him either, and for some reason the thought of that disturbed him. Then he thought of Caroline, and swallowed. Maybe, under the circumstances, that would be the best of the two options.

Alternatively, if he laughed it off—then some of this rapidly building tension might dissolve…

He relaxed and let his blue eyes crinkle at the corners. It was a calculated move because he knew only too well the effect that particular look had. It worked on everyone—men, women, children, animals. It was a charm he had in abundance, but he had never used it quite as deliberately as he did right now. 'Don't be absurd,' he denied softly. 'It was just a joke.'

'Pretty poor taste joke,' commented Holly, but it was

impossible not to thaw when confronted by that melting blue gaze.

'Listen, why don't I help you unload your roof-rack so that you can move your car more easily?' He smiled at her properly then, and Holly honestly couldn't think of a single objection.

CHAPTER TWO

'UNLESS,' Luke queried, blue eyes narrowing, 'you have someone else to help you?'

Holly shook her head. 'Nope. Just me. All on my own.'

'Well, then. Show me what needs doing.'

She looked into his eyes, confused by this sudden softening of his attitude towards her. One minute he was Mr Mean, the next he was laying on the charm with a trowel, and—surprise, surprise—he was very good at *that*! 'What's the catch?'

'No catch.'

'Well, that's very sweet of you—' she began, but he shook his head firmly.

'No, not sweet,' he corrected. 'I am never *sweet*, Holly.'

'What, then?' She wrinkled her nose at him. 'Let's go on what we know about you already. Kind? Polite? Gentlemanly?'

He laughed, and even that felt like a brief betrayal, until he told himself that he was being stupid. Men could be friends with women, couldn't they? Or, if not actually *friends*, then friend*ly*. Just because you had a laugh and a joke with a woman, it didn't mean that the two of you automatically wanted to start tearing each other's clothes off.

'Let's just say that it wouldn't rest very easily on my

conscience if I walked away knowing that I had left you to deal with that outrageous amount of luggage. I'm kind of old-fashioned like that.'

Holly regarded him steadily, but her heart was beating fast. She wasn't used to men coming out with ruggedly masculine statements like that last one. 'You mean that I'm too much of a delicate female to be able to ma-noeuvre a couple of suitcases off the roof-rack?'

'Delicate?' Luke looked her over very thoroughly, telling himself that *she* had asked the question, and therefore he needed to give it careful consideration.

She was getting on for six feet—tall for a woman—with correspondingly long limbs. She had legs like a thoroughbred, he thought, then wished he hadn't—long and supple legs that seemed to go all the way up to her armpits. She was slim and narrow-hipped, but not skinny in the way that tall women very often could be. And her breasts were almost shocking in their fullness—they looked curiously and beautifully at odds with her boyish figure. 'No,' he growled. 'I wouldn't call you delicate.'

She wondered if he had noticed that she was blushing. Maybe not. He hadn't exactly been concentrating on her *face*, now, had he? There had been something almost *anatomical* in the way he had looked at her. If any other man had stared at her body quite so blatantly, she suspected that she would have asked them to leave. But she didn't feel a bit like asking Luke to leave. With Luke she just wanted him to carry on looking at her like that all day long.

'So do you want my help, or not?'

Holly swallowed, wishing that everything he said didn't sound like a loaded and very sexy question. And the decision was really very simple—if she wanted to be totally independent and self-sufficient then she should decline his offer and do it all herself.

But a *sensible* person wouldn't do that, would they? After all, she knew no one here, not a soul. Was she, the great risk-taker, really tying herself up in knots over a simple offer of assistance just because it happened to come from a man she found overwhelmingly attractive? Wasn't that a form of sexism in itself?

'Thanks very much! You can start bringing the stuff in from the car, if you like,' she told him, trying to sound brisk and workmanlike, 'while I go and see how habitable it is upstairs. I just hope it's more promising than down here.' But her voice didn't hold out much hope. 'Unless you happen to have been up there lately?'

He shook his head. 'I've never set foot inside the place before.'

Holly frowned. 'But I thought you said you were the landlord?'

'I did. And I am—but an extremely *new* landlord. It's a long story.' He shrugged, in answer to the questioning look in her eyes. In the dim winter light shining through the shop window he became acutely conscious of how pale her skin looked, how bright her green eyes. With the deep copper ringlets tumbling unfettered around her shoulders, she could have stepped straight out of a pre-Raphaelite painting, jeans or no jeans, and he suddenly felt icy with a foreboding of unknown source.

'And you didn't ask to see any credentials,' he accused suddenly. 'Basic rule of safety, number one.' His eyes glittered. 'And you broke it.'

'Do you have any on you?'

'Well, no,' he admitted reluctantly. 'But the lesson is surely that I could be absolutely anyone—'

'The impostor landlord?' She hammed it up. 'About to hurl me to the floor and have your wicked way with me?'

The air crackled with tension. 'That isn't funny,' he said heavily.

'No,' she agreed, and her throat seemed to constrict as their gazes clashed. 'It isn't.'

'In fact, it's a pretty dumb thing to do—to put yourself in such a vulnerable situation,' he growled.

Independent and self-sufficient—huh! She had fallen headlong at the first hurdle. 'Okay. Okay. Lesson received and understood.'

He was still frowning. 'You'd better give me the keys,' he instructed tersely. 'And I'll move your car when I've unloaded all the stuff.'

Holly hesitated. 'Er—you might find she's a little temperamental in cold weather—like all cars of that age.'

'I should have guessed!' His voice was tinged with both irritation and concern—though he didn't stop to ask himself why. How was she hoping to get a business up and running if she was *this* disorganised? 'Why the hell don't you buy yourself a decent car?' he drawled. 'Didn't it occur to you that you might need something more reliable?'

His sentiments were no different from her own, but it was one thing deciding that she needed a newer car for herself—quite another for a complete stranger to bossily interrogate her on why she hadn't bought one!

'Of course it *occurred* to me,' she agreed. 'But reliable usually means boring. And expensive. To get an interesting car that you can count on costs a lot more money than I'm prepared or able to spend at the moment.' She gave him a reassuring smile. 'But don't worry if she won't start first time. A little coaxing usually works wonders.'

That smile was so *cute*. He threw her a lazy look in response. 'And I'm a dab hand at coaxing the temperamental.'

'Just cars?' she quizzed, before she could stop herself. 'Or women?'

He held her gaze in mocking query. 'Do you always make assumptions about people?'

'Everyone does. You did about me. And was my assumption so wrong?'

'In this case, it was. I was talking about coaxing horses, actually—not the opposite sex.'

He had hooked his fingers into the loops of his jeans as he spoke, and he suddenly looked all man—all cowboy. Holly nodded and bit back a smile. It all made sense now. He had looked completely wrong strolling down a sleepy English village street, with his jeans and battered sheepskin and tough good looks. But she could picture him on horseback—legs astride, the muscle and the strength of the man and the animal combining in perfect harmony. It was a powerful and earthy image and she found that persistent fingers of awareness were prickling down her back. 'Really?' She swallowed. 'Round here?'

'No. Not round here. I've only just got back from Africa.' He read the question in her eyes. 'It's a long story.'

That might explain the tan. 'Another one? So when did you get back?'

He glanced down at the watch on his wrist—a tough-looking timepiece which suited him well. 'About twelve hours ago.'

'Then you must be jet-lagged?'

'Yeah, maybe I am.' Could he blame this troublesome tension on jet-lag, he wondered, or would that be fooling himself? He took the keys from her unprotesting fingers. 'You go on up and I'll start moving the stuff.'

Masterful, thought Holly wistfully, then immediately felt guilty as she found the staircase at the back of the shop, which led directly to the flat upstairs. Masterful men were very passé these days, surely?

The stair carpet was worn, and upstairs the accommodation was basic—in a much worse state than the shop below. Holly sniffed. It had the sour, dark tang of a place unlived in.

She glanced around, trying to remember what had caught her enthusiasm in the first place. There was an okay-sized sitting room, whose window overlooked the street, a small bedroom containing a narrow and unwelcoming-looking bed, a bathroom with the obligatory dripping tap, and a kitchen which would have looked better in a museum. So far, so bad.

But it was the main bedroom which had first attracted her, and Holly sighed now with contentment as she looked at it again. Dusty as the rest of the apartment, it nonetheless was square and spacious, with a correspondingly high ceiling, and would be absolutely perfect as a workroom.

She heard footsteps on the stairs and went out to the landing to see Luke, with a good deal of her belongings firmly clamped to his broad shoulders.

She rescued a tin-opener which was about to fall out of an overfull cardboard box. 'You shouldn't carry all that!' she remonstrated. 'You'll do yourself damage.'

He barely looked up as he put down two big suitcases and brushed away a lock of the dark, gold-tipped hair which had fallen onto his forehead. 'Nice of you to be so concerned,' he said wryly. 'But I'm not stupid. And I'm used to carrying heavy weights around the place.'

She watched unobserved while he took the stairs back down, three at a time. Yes, he was. A man didn't get muscles like that from sitting behind a desk. Holly had grown up in the city, and city men were what she knew best. And they tended to have the too-perfect symmetry gained from carefully programmed sessions in the gym. Whereas those muscles looked natural. She swallowed. Completely natural.

It wasn't until he had done the fourth and final load, and dumped her few mismatched saucepans in the kitchen, that Luke stood back, took a good look around him and scowled.

'The place is absolutely disgusting! It's filthy! I wouldn't put a dog in here! Didn't you demand that it be cleaned up before you took possession?'

'Obviously not!' she snapped back.

'*Why* not?'

Because she had been blinded by the sun and by ambition? Mellowed by the gin and tonic which Doug Reasdale had given her, and an urgent need to get on with her life? 'I was just pleased to get a shop of this size for the money,' she said defensively.

His voice was uncompromising. 'It's a dump!'

'And I assumed that's why it was so cheap—I under-

stood that you took a property on as seen, and this was
how I saw it.'

'And who told you that? Doug?'

'That's right. But I checked it out afterwards, and he
was absolutely right.'

He laughed, but there was a steely glint in his eyes.
'Lazy bastard! I'll speak to him.'

'You don't have to do that,' she told him, with a shake
of her head. 'Like I said—I didn't exactly insist.'

'He took advantage of you,' he argued.

No, but he'd have liked to have done, thought Holly,
with a shudder.

'Sounds like you need a little brushing up on your
negotiation techniques.' He frowned as he looked
around, his mouth flattening with irritation. 'This place
is uninhabitable!'

As if on cue, a rattle of wind chattered against the
window-pane and raindrops spattered on the ledge. Luke
threw another disparaging glance around the room. On
closer inspection, there was a small puddle on the sill
where the rain obviously leaked through on a regular
basis.

'If I'd been around there is no way I would have let
you move into a place when it was in this kind of state.'

'Well, there's no point saying that now because you
weren't around,' she pointed out. 'Were you?'

'No.' God, no. But now he was.

Their eyes met again, and Luke tried to subdue the
magnetic pull of sexual desire. It had happened before—
this random and demanding longing—but never with
quite this intensity. It was sex, pure and simple. And it
meant nothing, not long term—he knew that. Its potency

and its allure would be reduced by exposure and it was completely unconnected with the real business of living, and relationships.

He should get out of here. Now. Away from those witchy green eyes and those soft lips which looked as if they could bring untold pleasure to a man's body.

Yet some dumb protective instinct reared its interfering head, and when he spoke he sounded like a man who'd already made his mind up. 'You can't stay here when it's like this.'

'I don't have a choice,' said Holly quietly.

There was a pause.

'Oh, yes, you do,' came his soft contradiction.

Holly stared at him in confusion, convinced by the dark look on his face that he was going to tell her to go back where she came from—back where she belonged. But this wasn't the Wild West, and she was a perfectly legitimately paid-up leaseholder of this flat! She gave a little smile. 'Really? And what's that?'

Luke wondered if he had just taken leave of his senses. 'Well, you could always come up to the house and stay with me,' he offered.

She searched his face. 'You're kidding!'

'Why should I be? I feel responsible—'

'Why should *you* feel responsible?'

'Because it's bleak and cold in here, and because the property is mine and I have enough bedrooms to cope with an unexpected guest.'

'But I don't even know you!'

He laughed. 'There's no need to make me sound like Bluebeard! And what's that got to do with anything?

You must have shared flats with men when you were a student, didn't you?'

'Doesn't everyone?'

'So how well did you know *them*?

'That's different.'

'How is it different?'

The difference was that none of her fellow design students—for all their velvet clothes and pretty-boy faces and extravagant gestures and prodigious talent—had appealed to Holly in any way that could be thought of as sexual. She had shared flats with men of whom she could honestly say it wouldn't have bothered her if they had strutted around the place stark naked. Whereas Luke Goodwin...

She thought of soft beds and central heating, and couldn't deny that she was tempted, but Holly shook her head. 'No, honestly, it's very kind of you to offer, but I'll manage.'

'How?'

'I'm resourceful.'

'You'll need to be,' he gritted, his eyes going to the grey circle of damp on the ceiling. 'I'll have someone fix that tomorrow.'

He started to move slowly towards the door, and Holly realised that she was as reluctant for him to leave as he appeared to be. 'Would you like some tea? As a kind of thank-you for helping me bring my stuff up?' she added quickly. 'And you're the one with the milk!'

'And the biscuits!' He found himself almost purring in the green dazzle of her eyes. 'That would be good.' He nodded, ignoring the logic which told him that he would be far wiser to get out now, while the going was good. 'I left them downstairs. I'll go and fetch them.'

The room seemed empty once he had gone, and Holly filled the kettle and cleared a space in the sitting room, dusting off the small coffee-table and then throwing open the window to try and clear the air.

But the chill air which blasted onto her face didn't take the oddly insistent heat away from her cheeks. She found herself wondering what subtle combination of events and chemistry had combined to make her feel so attracted to a man she had known less than an hour.

But by the time Luke returned with the milk and biscuits she had composed herself so that her face carried no trace of her fantasies, and her hand was as steady as a rock as she poured out two mugs of tea and handed him one.

'Thanks.' He looked around him critically. 'It's cold in here, too.'

'The window's open,' she said awkwardly.

'Yeah, I'd noticed.'

'I'll shut it.' The room now seemed so cramped, and he seemed so big in it. Like a full-sized man in a doll's house—and surely it wasn't just the long legs and the broad shoulders. Some people had an indefinable quality—some kind of magnetism which drew you to them whether you wanted it or not, and Luke Goodwin certainly had it in spades.

She perched on the edge of one of the overstuffed armchairs. 'So what were you doing in Africa?'

He cupped the steaming mug between strong, brown hands and stared into it. 'I managed a game reserve.'

Holly tried hard not to look too impressed. 'You make it sound like you were running a kindergarten!'

'Do I?' he mocked, his blue eyes glinting.

'A bit.' She crossed her legs. 'Big change of scenery. Do you like it?'

'Give me time,' he remonstrated softly, thinking that, when he looked at those sinfully long legs, he felt more alive than he had any right to feel. And the scenery looked very good from where he was sitting. 'Like I said—I just got in late last night.'

Holly found that breath suddenly seemed in very short supply. 'And are you here for…good?'

'That depends on how well I settle here.' He shrugged, and he screwed his eyes up, as if he were looking into the sun. 'It's been a long time since I've lived in England.'

She thought that he didn't sound as though he was exactly bursting over with enthusiasm about it. 'So why the upheaval? The big change from savannah to rural England?'

He hesitated as he wondered how much to tell her. His inheritance had been unexpected, and he had sensed that for some men in his situation it could become a burden. He was Luke—just that—always had been. But people tended to judge you by what you owned, not by what you were; he'd met too many women who had dollar signs where their eyes should be.

Yet it wasn't as though he feared being desired for money alone. He had had members of the opposite sex eating out of his hand since he was eighteen years old. With nothing but a pair of old jeans, a tee shirt and a backpack to his name, he had always had any woman he'd ever wanted. And a few he hadn't, to boot. Even so, it was important to him that he had known Caroline before he had inherited his uncle's estate. And what difference would it make if Holly Lovelace knew about his life and his finances? He wasn't planning to make her part of it, was he?

'Because my uncle died suddenly, and I am his sole heir.' He watched her very carefully for a reaction.

Holly's eyes widened. 'That sounds awfully grand.'

'I guess it is.' He sipped his tea. 'It was certainly unexpected. One morning I woke up to discover that I was no longer just the manager of one of the most beautiful game reserves in Kenya, but the owner of an amazing Georgian house, land and property dotted around the place, including this shop.'

'From ranch hand to lord of all he surveys?'

'Well, not quite.'

'But a big inheritance?'

'Sizeable.'

'And you're a wealthy man now?'

'I guess I am.'

So he had it all, Holly realised, simultaneously accepting that he was way out of her league—as if she hadn't already known that. There certainly weren't many men like Luke Goodwin around. He had good looks, physical strength and that intangible quality of stillness and contemplation which you often found in people who had worked the land. And now money, too. He would be *quite a catch.*

She let her eyes flicker quickly to his left hand and then away again before he could see. He wore no ring, and no ring had been removed as far as she could tell, for there wasn't a white mark against the tan of his finger.

'You aren't married?' she asked.

Straight for the jugular, he thought. Luke was aware of disappointment washing in a cold stream over his skin. He shook his tawny head. 'No, I'm not married.' But still he didn't mention Caroline. He could barely think straight in the green spotlight of her eyes. 'And now it's your turn.'

She stared at him uncomprehendingly. 'My turn?'

'Life story.' He flipped open the packet of biscuits and offered her one.

Holly gave a short laugh as she took one and bit into it. 'You call *that* a life story? You filled in *your* life in about four sentences.'

'I don't need to know who your best friend was in fifth grade,' he observed, only it occurred to him that 'need' was rather a strong word to have used, under the circumstances. 'Just the bare bones. Like why a beautiful young woman should take on a shop like this, in the middle of nowhere? Why Woodhampton, and not Winchester? Or even London?'

'Isn't it obvious? Because, unless you work for yourself, you have very little artistic control over your designs. If you work for someone else they always want to inject *their* vision, and their ideas. I've done it since I left art school and I've had enough.'

'You're very fortunate to be able to set up on your own so young,' he observed. 'Who's your backer?' Some oily sugar-Daddy, he'd bet. An ageing roué who would run his short, stubby fingers proprietorially over those streamlined curves of hers. Luke shuddered with distaste. But if that was the case—then where was he now?

'I don't have a backer,' she told him. 'I'm on my own.'

He stared at her with interest as all sorts of unwanted ideas about how she had arranged her finances came creeping into his head. 'And how have you managed that?'

She heard the suspicion which coloured his words. 'Because I won a competition in a magazine. I designed a wedding dress and I won a big cheque.'

Luke nodded. So she had talent as well as beauty. 'That was very clever of you. Weren't you tempted just to blow it?'

'Never. I didn't want to fritter the money away. I wanted to chase my dream—and my dream was always to make wedding dresses.'

'Funny kind of dream,' he observed.

'Not really—my mother did the same. Maybe it runs in families.'

She remembered growing up—all the different homes she'd lived in and all the correspondingly different escorts of her mother's. But her mother had always sewn—and even when she'd no longer had to design dresses to earn money she had done it for pleasure, making exquisite miniatures for her daughter's dolls. It had been one of Holly's most enduring memories—her mother's long, artistic fingers neatly flying over the pristine sheen of soft satin and Belgian lace. The rhythmic pulling of the needle and thread had been oddly soothing. Up and down, up and down.

'And why here?' He interrupted her reverie. 'Why Woodhampton?'

'Because I wanted an old-fashioned Georgian building which was affordable. Somewhere with high ceilings and beautiful dimensions—the kind of place that would complement the dresses I make. City rents are prohibitive, and a modern box of a place wouldn't do any justice to my designs.'

He looked around him with a frown. 'So when are you planning to open?'

'As soon as possible.' There was a pause. 'I can't afford not to.'

'How soon?'

'As soon as I can get the place straight. Get some pre-Christmas publicity and be properly established by January—that's when brides start looking for dresses in earnest.' She looked around her, suddenly deflated as the enormity of what she had taken on hit her, trying and failing to imagine a girl standing on a box, with yards of pristine ivory tulle tumbling down to the floor around her while Holly tucked and pinned.

'It's going to take a lot of hard work,' he observed, watching her frown, wondering if she had any real idea of how much she had taken on.

Holly was only just beginning to realise how much. 'I'm not afraid of hard work,' she told him.

Luke came to a sudden decision. He had not employed Doug Reasdale; his uncle had. But the man clearly needed teaching a few of the basic skills of management—not to mention a little compassion. 'Neither am I. And I think I'd better help you to get everything fixed, don't you? It's going to take for ever if you do it on your own.'

Holly's heart thumped frantically beneath her breast. 'And why would you do that?'

'I should have thought that was fairly obvious. Because I have a moral obligation, as your landlord. The place should never have been rented out to you in this condition.' And that much, at least, was true. He told himself that his offer had absolutely nothing to do with the way her eyes flashed like emeralds, her lips curved like rubies when she smiled that disbelieving and grateful smile at him. 'So what do you say?'

She couldn't think of a thing. She felt like wrapping her arms tightly around his neck to thank him for his generosity, but the thought of how he might react to that made her feel slightly nervous. There was something about Luke Goodwin which didn't invite affection from women. Sex, maybe, but not affection. 'What can I say?' she managed eventually. 'Other than a big thank you?'

'Promise me that if you can't cope, then you'll call on me.'

'But I don't know where you live.'

'Come here,' he said softly. He gestured for her to join him by the window, where the yellow light was fast fading like a dying match in the winter sky. He pointed. 'See that house through the arched hedge?'

It was difficult not to—the place was a mansion by most people's standards! 'That's *yours*?' she asked.

'Yes, it is. So if it all gets too much, or if you change your mind, then just walk on right up to the door and knock. Any time.' Blue eyes fixed her with their piercing blaze. 'And you'll be quite safe there—I promise. Okay?'

'Okay,' Holly agreed slowly, though instinct told her that seeking help from a man like Luke might have its own particular drawbacks.

CHAPTER THREE

As soon as Luke got home, he phoned Doug Reasdale, his late uncle's letting agent—a man he had just about been able to tolerate down the echoed lines of a long-distance phone call from Africa. He suspected that this time around he might have a little difficulty hanging onto his temper.

'Doug? It's Luke Goodwin here.'

'*Luke!*' oozed Doug effusively. 'Well, what do you know? Hi, man—how's it going? Good to have you back!'

'After sixteen years away, you mean?' observed Luke rather drily. He had met Doug once, briefly, when he had flown over for his uncle's funeral earlier in the year. Luke and the agent were about the same age, which Doug had obviously taken as a sign of true male camaraderie since he had spent the afternoon being relentlessly chummy and drinking whisky like water.

'It's actually very good to *be* back,' Luke said, realising to his surprise that he meant it.

'So what can I do you for?' quizzed Doug. 'House okay?'

'The house is fine. Beautiful, in fact.' He paused. 'I'm not ringing about the house.'

'Oh?'

'Does the name Holly Lovelace ring a bell?'

There was a low whistling noise down the phone.

42

'Reddish hair and big green eyes? Legs that go on for ever? Breasts you could spend the rest of your life dreaming about? Just taken over the lease of the vacant shop?' laughed Doug raucously. '*Tell* me about her!'

Luke's skin chilled and he was filled with an uncharacteristic urge to do violence. 'Is it customary to speak about leaseholders in such an over-familiar manner?' he asked coldly.

Doug clearly did not have the most sensitive antennae in the world. 'Well, no,' he admitted breezily. 'Not usually. But then they don't usually look like Holly Lovelace.' His voice deepened. 'Mind you—not that I think she's much of a goer—'

'I'm sorry?' Luke spoke with all the iced disapproval and disbelief he could muster.

'Well, she's got that kind of wild and free look—know what I mean? Wears those floaty kind of dresses—but oddly enough she was as prim as a nun the day I took her to lunch.'

'You took her out to *lunch*?' Luke demanded incredulously.

'Sure. Can you blame me?'

Luke ignored the question. 'And do you do that with all prospective leaseholders?'

'Well, no, actually.' Doug gave a nervous laugh. 'But, like I said, she's not someone you'd forget in a hurry.'

Luke forced himself to concentrate on the matter in hand, and not on how much he was going to enjoy firing his land agent once he had found a suitable replacement. 'What do you think of the current condition of the property, Doug?'

Another nervous laugh. 'It's been empty for ages.'

'I'm not surprised, and that doesn't really answer my question—what do *you* think of the condition?'

'It's basic,' Doug admitted. 'But that's why she got it so cheap—'

'*Basic?* The place is a slum! The roof in the upstairs flat is leaking,' he said coldly. 'Were you aware?'

'I knew there—'

'The window-frames are ill-fitting and the furniture looks like it's been salvaged from the local dump,' interrupted Luke savagely. 'I want everything fixed that can be fixed, and replaced if it can't. And I want it done yesterday!'

'But that's going to cost you *money*!' objected Doug. 'A lot of money.'

'I'd managed to work that out for myself,' drawled Luke.

'And it's going to eat into your profit margins, Luke.'

Luke kept his voice low. 'I don't make profit on other people's misery or discomfort,' he said. 'And I don't want a woman staying in a flat that is cold and damp. If she gets cold or gets sick, then it isn't going to be on *my* conscience. Got that?'

'Er—got it,' said Doug, and began to chew on a fingernail.

'How soon can it be done?'

Doug thought of local decorators who owed him; carpenters who would be pleased to work for the new owner of Apson House. Maybe it was time to call in a few favours. And he suspected that his job might be on the line if he didn't come up with something sharpish. 'I can have it fixed in under a month!' he hazarded wildly.

'Not good enough!' Luke snapped.

'But good craftsmen get booked up ages in advance,' objected Doug.

'Then pay them enough so that they'll *un*book!'

'Er—right. Would a fortnight be okay?'

'Is that a definite?'

'I'll make sure it is,' promised Doug nervously.

'Just do that!' And Luke put the phone down roughly in its cradle.

Holly washed out the two mugs she and Luke had used, put them on the drainer to dry, then set about trying to make the place halfway habitable before all the thin afternoon light faded from the sky.

The 'hot' water was more tepid than hot, so she boiled up a kettle, added the water to plenty of disinfectant and cleaning solution in a bucket, and began to wipe down all the surfaces in the kitchen. Next she scrubbed the bathroom from top to bottom, until her fingers were sore and aching and she thought she'd better stop. Her hands were her livelihood and she had to look after them.

She sat back on her heels on the scruffy linoleum floor and wondered how many kettles of water it would take to fill the bath. Too many! she thought ruefully. She had better start boiling now, and make her bed up while she was waiting.

She gathered together clean sheets and pillowcases and took them into the bedroom, and was just about to make a start when she noticed a dark patch on the mattress and bent over to examine it. Closer inspection revealed that it was nothing more sinister than water from a tiny leak in the ceiling, but she couldn't possibly sleep on a damp mattress—which left the floor.

She bit her lip, trying not to feel pathetic, but she was close to tears and it was no one's fault but her own. Not only had she stupidly rented a flat which looked like a slum, but she had brought very little in the way of entertainment with her, and even the light was too poor to sew by. The only book in her possession was some depressing prize-winner she had been given as a present before she left, and a long Sunday evening yawned ahead of her. And now she couldn't even crash out at the earliest opportunity because the bed was uninhabitable!

So, did she start howling her eyes out and opt for sleeping on the floor? Or did she start acting like a modern, independent woman, and take Luke Goodwin up on his offer of a bed?

Without giving herself time to change her mind, she pulled on a sweater, bundled on a waterproof jacket, and set off to find him.

Luke was sitting at the desk in the first-floor study, working on some of his late uncle's papers, when a movement caught his attention, and he started with guilty pleasure, his eyes focussing in the gloomy light as he saw Holly walk through the leafy arch towards his house.

He watched her closely. With her long legs striding out in blue denim, she looked the epitome of the modern, determined woman. And so at odds with the fragility of her features, the wild copper confusion of the hair which the winter wind had whipped up in a red storm around her face.

He ran downstairs and pulled the front door open before she'd even had time to knock. He saw that she was white-faced with fatigue, and the dark smudges underneath the eyes matched the dusty marks which were painted on her cheeks like a clown. Again, that unwanted feeling of protectiveness kicked in like a mule. That and desire.

For a split second he felt the strongest urge to just shut the door in her face, telling himself that he was perfectly within his rights to do so. That he owed her nothing. But then her dark lashes shuddered down over the slanting emerald eyes and he found himself stepping back like a footman.

'Changed your mind about staying?' he asked softly, though he noticed that she carried no overnight bag.

'I had it changed for me,' she told him unsteadily. 'And you're right—it *is* a dump! There's no hot water, there's a big patch of damp on the mattress and springs sticking through it! And before you point anything else out, I admit I should have checked it out better—insisted it be cleaned out before my arrival, or something. *And* I came ill prepared. No radio, no television, and the only book I brought with me is buried at the bottom of a suitcase I daren't unpack because there's nowhere to put anything! Just don't make fun of me, Luke, not tonight—because I don't think I can cope with it.'

He heard the slight quaver in her voice and saw the way her mouth buckled into a purely instinctive little pout. He thought how irresistible she was, with her powerful brand of vulnerability coupled with that lazy-eyed sensuality. 'Come in,' he growled quietly, and held the door open for her. 'I have no intention of making fun of you. I'd much rather you came here than have you suffering in silence.'

'Would you? Honestly?'

'Yes,' he lied, as he felt his pulse drumming heavily against the thin skin around his temple. Irresistibly, he let his eyes drift over her. 'You look like you could use a hot tub—or maybe you'd prefer a drink first?'

'That's real fairy-godmother language.' She smiled at him, thankful that he hadn't seen fit to deliver another lecture. 'I'd like the hottest, deepest bath on offer!'

'A bath it is, then. Come upstairs with me.' His eyes glinted with humour. 'God—I *do* sound like Bluebeard, don't I?'

'Who *is* this Bluebeard?' she quizzed mischievously, her eyes sparking as she followed him upstairs, automatically running a slow finger along the gleaming bannister. 'Nice staircase.'

Nice house in general. It soon became obvious that no money had been spared in modernising the place. The paintwork was clean and sparkling and the floorboards had been polished to within an inch of their lives.

He led her to the biggest bathroom Holly had ever seen, with an elegant free-standing bath painted a deep cobalt blue, and enough bottles of scent and bath essence to start a *parfumerie*. He pulled open the door to an airing cupboard where soft piles of snowy towels lay stacked on shelves.

Holly looked round her with pleasure, feeling like Cinderella. 'Mmm! Sybaritic!'

'Did you bring anything to change into?' he asked abruptly.

'You mean—like pyjamas?'

He found that he couldn't look her in the eye; the thought of her in pyjamas—or, even worse, *not* in pyjamas—was distracting to say the least. Bizarrely, he felt the hot hardening of an erection begin to stir, and he forced himself to channel the desire into something less threatening—like irritation. 'I meant some different clothes—the ones you have on are filthy.'

Holly heard the undisguised disapproval in his voice and stared down at herself, at the dusty jeans and spattered sweater, the dirt beneath her broken fingernails. He was right—she looked like a tramp. She shook her head and damp tendrils snaked exotically around her face. 'No, I didn't.' She gave him a rueful look. 'It might have looked a little pushy if I'd turned up on your doorstep with a suitcase!'

It certainly wouldn't have been very beneficial to his blood pressure. 'I can loan you a dressing gown,' he told her evenly. 'And put everything else in the washing machine. It'll be clean and dry in a couple of hours. Leave it outside the door and I'll see to it. You can fetch your other clothes in the morning.'

'You're very kind,' said Holly, meaning it.

'Am I?' His voice was mocking, but then 'kind' wasn't an adjective he usually associated with himself. Certainly not where women were concerned. He watched as she shrugged out of her oilskin jacket and draped it over the back of a chair. 'It's all yours,' he told her, and decided to absent himself as quickly as possible—his mind was already working overtime as he imagined her wriggling her jeans off and sliding her panties down over those long, long legs. Always presuming she was wearing any… 'Take as long as you like.'

'I will,' she smiled, and shut the door behind him.

It was possibly the best bath of Holly's life. She

squirted jasmine and tuberose into the water and, when the bubbles had nearly reached the top, she climbed in and closed her eyes and tried to relax. She couldn't do *anything* about a damp mattress right now—so the most sensible thing would be to put it out of her mind altogether.

She had been in there for the best part of an hour, dreaming up a frothy white bridal petticoat inspired by the fragrant bubble bath, when there was a rapping on the door and she heard Luke's deep voice outside.

'You haven't fallen asleep, have you?'

She stirred in the water. Her flesh had deepened to rose-pink in the warmth, and the buds of her nipples instantly began tightening to the velvet caress of his voice. 'N-not yet, I haven't!' Shakily, she turned the tap on and flicked some cold water onto her burning skin.

'Then come and have something to drink. I've left you a robe outside.'

It was pure heaven to slide the soft white towelling robe on and knot it tightly around her narrow waist. She brushed her hair and left it, still damp and flapping around her shoulders, as she went in search of Luke.

He was sitting on the floor by a roaring fire in the first-floor drawing room, a tray of tea in front of him, half-read newspapers at his side. He watched as she came in, noticing how the pure white of the robe emphasised the firelight-red of her hair, while the soft fluffy material accentuated the carved delicacy of her bone structure. She looked a creature of contrasts, midway between angel and imp.

A pulse flickered at his temple and he felt the blood begin to pound in his head, but *he* had been the one who had invited her here. Was he crazy, or *what*? 'Would you like some tea?' he said evenly.

'Please.'

'How do you like it?'

'Just milk—no sugar.' She took the cup he handed her and sat in front of the fire, folding her long legs up beneath her and then carefully tucking the robe closely around her thighs until she saw him watching her, and stopped. She had meant to *cover* her legs, not draw attention to them.

Luke watched the flicker of amber and copper as the firelight danced across her face and wondered why he felt this random longing for her. Because of the apparent contradiction of her looks? Those sensual movements of the born siren—made all the more potent by that startled look of wide-eyed innocence she must have spent years perfecting?

His voice was a growl. 'Why don't you bring your tea through to the kitchen—I'm just about to make something to eat. I'm starving,' he lied. 'And you must be, too. Unless you brought provisions with you, which, judging by your general standards of preparation, I doubt.'

Holly felt too flustered by the way he had been looking at her to even bother acknowledging the criticism. Food was the very last thing on her mind, even though it had been hours since breakfast, when she'd eaten a banana on the run. But food would be a distraction, and Holly sorely needed something to distract her from those amazing blue eyes, and from the underlying tension which was crackling through the air like sparks from a newly lit bonfire. And besides, if they didn't eat, there was one hell of a long evening to get through...

'Starving,' she echoed dutifully. 'But surely there's no food if you arrived in the middle of the night?'

'I wasn't proposing anything fancy,' he drawled. 'But the freezer was filled in any case,' he explained. 'In time for my arrival.'

'How luxurious.'

'Yes,' he replied shortly.

Caroline again, of course, smooth and efficient. 'I know a company who will fill it for you,' she had told him briskly. 'With enough of the kind of food you like to see you through until I arrive.' She had playfully tapped the end of his nose with one of her professionally manicured nails. Caroline had smooth and beautiful hands, white and soft and unlined. 'Because we can't have you starving, can we, my darling?'

Luke found himself sneaking a glance at Holly's hands, as if to reassure himself of their unsuitability. *Her* nails were short, two were broken, two looked bitten and there were calluses on her palms.

The kitchen was downstairs, in the basement, and it looked as if it had been lifted from an illustration in a lifestyle magazine. It had been, as was the trend, 'sympathetically modernised'. There were light, carved wooden cupboards, and marble surfaces for chopping things, which even Holly—who could barely tell one end of a leek from another—could see were about as up-market as you could get. At the far end of the room was a fireplace piled with apple-wood logs, which glowed like amber, with two squashy-looking chairs on either side.

She sat down next to the fire and shook her damp hair out, watching while he began to boil up pasta and heat through a sauce.

'Like a beer?' he asked.

'Love one.'

He opened two bottles and handed her one, and she sipped it while he strained the pasta and stirred the sauce and pushed a bowl full of freshly grated Parmesan into the centre of the table.

'You look like a man who knows his way round a kitchen,' she observed slowly.

He shrugged. 'I'm used to fending for myself.'

'I thought people had lots of help in Africa?'

His smile was arcane. 'Some people do. I chose not to—just help with the cleaning, same as here. A woman named Margaret starts in the morning—I guess I'd better warn her that I have company.' He gave the sauce a final stir. 'I always think that, if you don't cook for yourself, then you lose touch with reality.' He looked up to where she sat, looking at him intently, and he thought that reality seemed a long way away at this precise moment.

Soon he had heaped two plates with pasta and sauce and they ate at the table in front of the fire.

Forcing himself to eat, Luke struggled to free himself from his rather obsessive study of the way the firelight warmed her skin tones into soft apricot and cream, casting around for something to say. Something which might make him forget that she was a very beautiful woman. 'So what were you doing before you came to Woodhampton?'

She shot him a half-amused glance. 'Just checking

that you haven't given refuge to some gun-toting ma-niac?'

'We could always talk about the weather, if you pre-fer,' he told her deliberately. 'But we have a whole eve-ning to get through.'

So they did. Holly took a hasty sip of her beer. It was difficult to concentrate when those amazing blue eyes were fixed on her with such interest. 'After school I went to art school, where I studied textile and design.'

'And were you a model student?' he mocked.

Holly frowned. 'Actually, I *was*, now you come to mention it. And I get a little fed up with people thinking that, just because a person is *creative*, they're automat-ically a lazy slob—'

'I doubt whether a lazy slob would go to the trouble of starting up their own business,' he put in drily.

'No, they wouldn't.' Feeling slightly mollified, Holly put her beer bottle back down on the table. 'I got quite a good degree—'

'And are you being modest now?'

Her eyes threw him a challenge. 'Mmm! I'm trying—'

'Very trying,' he agreed, deadpan.

'After I left college I went to work for the same fash-ion house which had employed my mother, but I hated it.'

'Why?'

'Because I felt exactly like an employee, with little control over the entire design process—not really. I felt like I was working in a factory, and I didn't want to be. I wanted to feel creatively free. So I entered the com-petition.' A dreamy smile came over her face as she remembered. 'And won.'

'Tell me about it,' he said, aware that his voice was unusually indulgent—but that kind of sweet enthusiasm would have melted the hardest heart.

Holly finished a mouthful of tagliatelle and looked into his eyes. Such gorgeous eyes. 'It was organised by one of the glossy bridal magazines to celebrate twenty-five years in publishing.' She met his blank stare. 'You know the kind of thing.'

'Not really,' he demurred, and gave a sardonic shake of his golden-brown head. 'Don't forget I've been living in the wilds all these years—and bridal magazines are pretty thin on the ground!'

Holly got a sudden and disturbingly attractive image of Luke Goodwin wearing a morning suit. 'The idea was to create a wedding dress for the new century—'

'So, let me guess—you did something wild and un-traditional?'

She shook her head slowly. 'No, I didn't, actually. Brides usually don't want to be too wild and wacky. Most conform. In fact, I based the dress on an idea that my mother had.' She saw his puzzled look. 'She was a dress designer, too,' she explained. 'She created this most wonderful wedding dress when I was little—I've seen pictures of it.'

'But if yours is almost the same as hers, isn't that called copying—even stealing?'

She shook her head. 'There's no such thing as origi-nality in fashion—you must know that. What goes around comes around. My design was very similar to my mother's but it wasn't *exactly* the same. Un-fortunately, Mum's dress was sold, and we never saw it again.'

Luke frowned. 'Why would you expect to?'

'Because she designed it for a very famous fashion house, and those types of garments don't usually disappear without trace. They're usually worth a lot of money.'

'But this one did?'

Holly nodded. 'Someone bought it in a sale. My mother was disappointed it was reduced in price, but not surprised—' Her face lit up with enthusiasm. 'It was a very unusual design, and only an exceptionally thin woman could have worn it. And that was that. Funnily enough, an older Irish woman who cleaned in the store where it was sold—she bought it. After that it disappeared into thin air.'

Luke was more interested in the things she *didn't* say than in the things she did. 'And where's your mother now?'

'Well, it's November, so she's probably in the Caribbean,' replied Holly flippantly. 'Either that, or on a cruise ship somewhere.'

The bitterness in her tone didn't escape him. 'And why isn't she here—helping her daughter get settled into her brand-new business venture?'

'Because her latest disgusting rich old husband probably won't let her,' grimaced Holly.

'Oh, it's like that, is it?' he queried softly.

She threw him a look, a nonchalant expression which had become second nature to her. At school she had quickly learnt that if you learned to mock yourself, then no one else would bother. 'Doesn't *everyone* have a mother who uses a man as a meal ticket?'

'You must hate it,' he observed slowly.

Holly shrugged. 'I'm used to it—she's used men all her life. But I'm not complaining—not really. Their money paid for my education, saw me through art school.'

'And wasn't there a father on the scene?'

'No, I never knew my father—' Holly met his curious stare with a proud uptilt to her chin, feeling oddly compelled to answer his questions. Maybe it was something to do with the penetrating clarity of his blue eyes. Or maybe it was just because he actually looked as though he *cared*.

She ran a finger down the cold beer bottle. 'And no, I'm afraid that it's nothing heroic like an early death— I mean it literally. My mother didn't know him either. According to her, he could have been one of two people and she didn't care for either of them—so she never bothered to tell either of them that she was pregnant.'

Luke expelled a slow breath of air. *'Hell,'* he said quietly, realising that he didn't have the monopoly on unconventional childhoods.

'I suppose I must be grateful that she saw fit to give birth to me.' Her gaze was unblinking. 'Have I shocked you?'

'A little,' he admitted. 'But that was part of your intention, wasn't it, Holly—to shock me?'

She looked at up at him, her eyes partially shaded by thick dark lashes. 'And why would I want to do that?'

'Because illegitimacy hasn't always been accepted the way it is now. When you were growing up, it was probably even a stigma—something to be ashamed of. Wasn't it?' he probed gently.

The memory of it was like a knife, twisting softly in

her belly. Little girls taunting her in the playground. The sense of always being different. 'Yes.'

Her reply was so quiet that he had to strain his ears to hear it. 'So maybe you got used to relating the facts as starkly as possible—to pre-empt that kind of reaction. And if *you* said the worst possible things about not having a father, then that way no one could hurt you. Or judge you.' He paused, and the piercing blue eyes were as direct as twin swords. 'Am I right?'

She put her fork down quickly. 'Yes, you're right.' He was very perceptive. *Too* perceptive. 'I don't know why I'm telling you all this,' she said. 'Just because you've been a Good Samaritan. I don't normally open up to people I've only just met, you know.'

He smiled through the ache that had haunted him since he had first laid eyes on her. 'Maybe it's *because* we're strangers. And because we've been thrown together in bizarre circumstances.'

'What's that got to do with anything?'

'Like people trapped in lifts, or stuck on the side of a mountain—that sense of isolation makes the rest of the world seem unimportant. You break rules.' He looked at her thoughtfully. 'Sometimes you make new ones in their place.'

Holly badly needed to distract herself—wasn't he *aware* that when he looked at her that way she just wanted him to kiss her? 'I may have told you things about *me*,' she corrected him. 'But it hasn't been very reciprocal. You've told me very little about *you*!'

'There's my inheritance,' he said blandly. 'You know about that.'

'Oh, *that*!' she scoffed. 'That's *boring*! I want to hear

about *real* life.' She tried an impersonation of his distinctive drawl. 'Life on the ranch!'

He laughed. It would be so easy to stay here, to bask in the firelight and the soft, green light of her eyes. Easy and dangerous...

'It's late and it'll keep,' he said, swallowing the last of his beer and wondering why it tasted so sour. 'And if I tell you about cheetah kills before bedtime—then you might have nightmares, mightn't you?'

'I suppose so!' She laughed nervously.

But then, Holly suspected that she might have trouble sleeping in any case. Because surely the thought of a big, virile man like Luke Goodwin sleeping in the same house would cause *any* normal woman to be restless.

Especially a woman whose green-eyed and naturally foxy appearance often gave people a totally misleading view of her true nature...

CHAPTER FOUR

DESPITE her reservations, Holly slept soundly and undisturbed in a beautiful high-ceilinged bedroom painted in palest blues and greys. It overlooked the rain-soaked lawn at the back of the house, which sloped down to a fruit orchard at the far end of the garden.

When she woke up it was almost nine, and she stretched luxuriously in the bed, rubbing her sleepy eyes as she threw back the duvet and padded over to the window.

The garden was like an illustration from a child's story book, and Holly could almost imagine the trees being able to speak, the fruits full of enchantment.

Her room had its own bathroom, a luxury she decided she would *never* take for granted! She showered and washed her hair again, put on Luke's white towelling gown, and was just thinking about going in search of her clothes when there was a rap on the door and she opened it to find him standing there, his eyes all shadowed, as though sleep had been at a premium.

His hair was still damp from the shower and he was dressed casually—still in a pair of faded blue denims with a thick, navy sweater pulled down low onto his hips.

'Hello, Holly,' he said softly, and just the sight of her stirred the memories of erotic dreams which had given him one of the worst nights in memory. 'Sleep well?'

She beamed at him with a sunny smile. 'Like a log!'

'Lucky you,' he commented drily, seeing the way her fingers fumbled to tighten the belt of her robe, or rather *his* robe, and he quickly held out her clean jeans, shirt and underwear. 'Thought you might need these. Washed and folded.'

She took the stack of neatly folded clothes from him, and looked down at them in surprise. 'I'm impressed,' she murmured.

Luke's eyes danced at her. 'Real men don't fold clothes, right? That's your stereotype?'

'I don't know enough game reserve managers-cum-lords of the manor to have formed a stereotype! But if ever times are hard—you could always find work in a laundry!'

She hugged the pile of clothes to her like a hot-water bottle, but the movement caused her black lace panties to dangle from the middle of the pile, and she realised that he must have folded *those*, too—as well as her jeans!'

'I'd better get dressed,' she said indistinctly.

'I'll have breakfast ready in ten minutes.'

'I don't generally eat breakfast.'

'I can tell.' Blue eyes roved over her narrow hips critically. 'Bad idea. The brain and the body need fuel after fasting overnight. You'll feel better for it. *Trust* me, Holly!'

Holly laughed as she shut the door on him. That was the oddest thing. She *did*! And, after the succession of doubtful escorts which her mother had trailed through her life, she didn't give her trust easily—certainly not to virtual strangers. Though when you'd shared a house with a man for the night, and he had washed and folded your underwear, then he hardly qualified as a stranger any more, did he?

She quickly put the clothes on, then went downstairs to find him.

He was standing in the kitchen, frying rashers of bacon on the Aga, and the aroma made her mouth water.

'That smells *wonderful*!' she confessed weakly.

He glanced up from flipping a rasher over in the pan.

'Sit down and have some juice,' he instructed, thinking that this was the first time he had ever cooked a woman breakfast without having had sex with her. He watched her intently reading the label of a marmalade jar. 'There's coffee in the pot—unless you'd rather have tea?'

She shook her head. The coffee smelt good, too. Far too good to refuse—hot and strong and black. 'Mmm. Bliss,' she told him, taking a sip.

'I make the best coffee in the world,' he said, with a not-so-modest shrug of his shoulders. 'Or so I'm told.'

'And there's your laundry skills. Tell me—is there no end to your talents?' she teased.

Well, there was something he'd been told he was *very* good at. There was a brief moment of silence while Luke bit back the temptation to look directly into her eyes and tell her exactly what it was…

'Have some toast,' he said abruptly as he put her food down in front of her.

It was the first time for as long as she could remember that Holly had sat down to a proper breakfast. She surveyed the plate piled with egg, bacon, mushrooms, tomatoes and beans, while Luke slipped in across the table opposite her.

'And where did all this food come from?' she wanted to know. 'Not the freezer?'

'No. While you were sleeping I went shopping—'

'You should have woken me,' she said automatically.

'What for? You looked like you needed the sleep.'

'I did.' Holly glanced around the kitchen as she finished a mouthful of bacon. Last night it had been dark, and she had been unable to properly appreciate the beauty of her surroundings. Through the French doors which opened out onto the garden she could see a winter-flowering blossom tree, its buds beginning to reveal the ice-pink petals which lay beneath.

It was so comfortable here, Holly thought. She leaned back in her chair and looked at him, trying to sound as though she minded the delay. 'And heaven knows how long it will take to get the shop looking habitable!'

'Two weeks, I've been told,' he offered drily. 'And that's going to be cutting it fine.'

'But I can't stay here for two weeks!'

Luke sipped his coffee, the cloud of steam obscuring the expression in his eyes. 'Have a problem with that, do you, Holly?'

'I'll get in your way—'

'No, you won't. I won't let you. I have a lock on my study door,' he grinned wolfishly.

Holly shrugged, the idea appealing more by the minute. 'It just seems a long time for me to impose on your hospitality—but if you're happy—'

'I don't know whether *happy* is the adjective I would have selected,' he observed drily. 'I had planned to spend the next couple of weeks sorting out my uncle's affairs—not entertaining a house guest.' Especially such a nubile house guest.

'Oh, but I won't need any entertaining!' she assured him. 'I've got masses to do myself. Paperwork and sewing and finding a florist I can work with. I'll keep out of your way. I promise.' It was no idle threat, either. Luke was an unsettling man, tempting and disturbing—and Holly needed that kind of distraction like a hole in the head right now.

He hoped she meant it. Lending her that bathrobe had been a bad idea. In fact, even *thinking* about that bathrobe was a bad idea. 'I've been on the phone to Doug again this morning. Who assured me that the structural repairs can be done inside forty-eight hours.' He glanced at his watch. 'Someone will be seeing to that roof right now.'

'Thank God for that!'

'Yeah,' he agreed blandly. 'Which just leaves decor. If you let me know your colour choices, I'll make sure that it gets done.'

Holly put her fork down and stared at him. 'But I thought that *I'd* be expected to decorate?'

Luke was keen not to come over as a completely soft touch. He told himself that he would behave in exactly the same way if the tenant happened to be a man. 'And so you would, if the condition of the place wasn't so disgusting—if it was just a question of cosmetics. But, since it needs more than a face-lift, I'll agree to decorate it to your specifications. How about fresh white paint everywhere? Sound okay?'

There was a pause. Holly pulled a face. 'Well, no. Now you come to mention it—not really.'

Denim-blue eyes narrowed. 'Oh?'

She pushed her plate aside, and leaned across the table towards him. 'I don't want to sound ungrateful, or anything, Luke—but what I envisaged as a colour scheme was something much more dramatic than that. Everyone else is doing white walls and big green plants in pots. But this is going to be the kind of bridal shop that no one will ever forget.'

He didn't react. 'Go on.'

'I wanted a deep, peacock-green wall.'

Luke noted her use of the singular. 'That's only one wall,' he commented.

Sharp of him. She drew in a deep breath, determined that he would be able to visualise the vibrant combinations of colours she had in mind. 'That's right—three walls and one window. I'd like another painted in that very rich, intense, almost royal purple—you know the shade.'

'And the final wall?' he queried, deadpan. 'What plans did you have for that—sky-blue pink?'

'Gold.' The same glossy gold which touched the tips of his hair.

'Gold?'

'Mmm.' Holly nodded her head enthusiastically. 'It's the perfect wedding colour—it symbolises the ring and it suggests pageantry and ceremony. And I want this shop to really stand out!'

He fleetingly wished that she wouldn't move with such a refreshing lack of inhibition when she got carried away like that. If only she'd wear a bra. Didn't she realise how ripe and how luscious such sudden movements could make her breasts appear? The hint of their succulent swell against the simple shirt she wore seemed positively indecent.

He swallowed down the erotic fantasies which were beginning to burgeon into life again. 'Stand out?' he quizzed mockingly, reflecting that it was a poor choice of phrase, given the circumstances. 'It will certainly do that!' He frowned. 'Though won't using specialist paints delay your opening—since I imagine that you'll have to buy the more unusual materials in London?'

Holly shook her head with a smile. 'Ah, but that's where you're wrong! There's a specialist paint shop right in Winchester—we need look no further than there!'

We.

Her easy use of the word caused Luke a moment of chilly disquiet, until he silently chided himself for his out-and-out arrogance. Was he now worried that Holly was getting possessive, or passionate, about him? When there had been *nothing* in his behaviour—not a word nor a gesture—which she could have interpreted or misinterpreted as some kind of come-on.

Holly saw the way his shoulders stiffened, and she could sense immediately what he was thinking. Her fingers crept up to cover her mouth apologetically. 'I'm sorry—I didn't mean to be presumptuous.'

He shook his head. 'You weren't being presumptuous. And we'll both go into Winchester to choose your paint.' After all, *he* was the one who was paying for them!

'But aren't you…?' She found that her words were tripping over themselves, as though they couldn't quite decide in what order to leave her mouth. 'Wouldn't you…?'

He looked into her widened green eyes with something approaching amusement. 'Wouldn't I what, Holly?'

'Wouldn't you rather be doing something else?'

He most certainly would.

Her words created such a shockingly graphic image in his mind that Luke briefly closed his eyes in despair. It was simply sexual attraction, he told himself over and over again, as if repetition would make it more believable. Nothing more than that—a combustive hormonal reaction which she had provoked in him, and which would fade as inevitably as the sunlight would fade from the afternoon sky. Was *she* aware of it, too? he wondered. Did it pulse and hum around *her*, too—the feeling almost palpable?

His mistake had been to take her into his house in the first place. To rush in playing the Good Samaritan, trying to fool himself into minimising the potency of the attraction he felt towards her—as if, by rationalising it, it would go away of its own accord.

Because it wasn't conveniently disappearing, and he somehow doubted that it would—unless you took sexual attraction through to its natural conclusion, which he had no intention of doing. For how could it disappear, if she continued to haunt him with those emerald eyes and that pale skin, and the careless cascade of coppery curls?

Maybe she was destined to always be one of those 'if only' women—if only he'd met her when he'd been in that sowing wild oats stage of his life. Holly Lovelace was enchantingly beautiful with her wild, artistic looks—great for a tempestuous affair, but...

The sooner she was set up in her newly decorated shop and out of his life, the better—and, just in case he was forgetting, he wasn't in the market for a lover.

'There's nothing else I'd rather be doing,' he lied. 'And besides, Margaret is coming in to clean the house this morning, so we'll leave for Winchester just as soon as you're ready.'

Winchester was crowded.

Luke looked at the throbbing crowds in disbelief. 'Where's the execution?'

'Sorry?'

'I mean, why else could all these people be here?'

'They're Christmas shoppers,' explained Holly, craning her neck to gaze up in awe at the cathedral.

'But it's only November!' he scowled.

'And some people buy their Christmas presents throughout the year. Apparently,' she added hastily, in case he thought that she was among them!

Luke stared at the looped ropes of fairy lights which twinkled in one shop window, surrounding the puffy cheeks of a beaming cardboard Santa. The same compilation tape of Christmas songs seemed to be blasting out of every shop they passed. He shook his head and thought longingly of the stark beauty of Africa. 'It's crazy—*crazy*—this whole commercial Christmas trip! A celebration of consumption and consumerism!'

Holly shrugged, pleased to hear his views echoing her own. 'I know. I keep planning to go into hibernation!'

They passed a florist's, where pots of fragrant winter

jasmine were stacked next to the gaudy crimson of the seasonal poinsettias. Luke saw a wreath—glossy green and spiky, and studded with berries the colour of blood. Ignoring the appreciative ogling of a young assistant through the window, he slowed down.

'I guess it's your birthday soon?' he hazarded.

Holly blinked. 'How did you know *that*?' she demanded, and then laughed as she looked down and spotted the holly wreath. *'Oh!'*

'Well, it's a Christmas name, isn't it?' He looked at her, a question in his eyes. 'Usually.'

'Yes, you're right. I was born on Christmas Eve.'

'"The night before Christmas?"' he quoted softly, until something in her eyes made him ask, 'But you don't enjoy your birthday?'

Maybe other men had always just asked the wrong questions in the past. Or maybe this man just asked the right ones. Whatever his gift, Holly found that she wanted to tell him things—personal things—in a way which was definitely *not* her usual style.

'No, I don't,' she told him slowly. 'Or, rather, I didn't—not when I was little. It's a difficult night of the year to get a babysitter—a fact that my mother never failed to remind me of. When I was older, she used to leave me while she went out, and in a way I preferred that. Less pressure—'

'How old?' he interrupted savagely.

Holly thought back. 'Ten. Eleven. But people weren't so paranoid about leaving children then,' she added hastily, as some innate loyalty to her mother made her want to defend her.

'And did you get presents?'

'Oh, yes. Huge presents sometimes—if the boyfriend was rich enough. Other years they were a little thin on the ground.'

He said something very soft beneath his breath.

Holly dodged a shopper who was steaming down the high street like a Sherman tank and sneaked a glance at Luke's hard profile. 'So how did you spend your Christmases in Africa?'

His mouth tightened as he found himself reluctant to *think* about it—let alone talk about it. Last Christmas he had spent with Caroline. She had flown in from Durban and had managed to create a traditional turkey dinner on his antiquated old stove. She had even brought linen napkins in her suitcase, and her gift to him had been fine crystal glasses, out of which they had drunk champagne, although his throat had been so dry with the heat that he would have preferred beer. She had raised her glass to him and, in that freeze-framed moment, had seemed to personify calm. An oasis in the hurly-burly of what his life had been up until that point. She had talked wistfully of the babies she longed to have, and everything had suddenly seemed to make perfect sense.

He'd remembered fragments of a conversation he had once had with an Indian friend, and these had drifted back to him as he'd stared into Caroline's serene face. It had been one of those East versus West debates. Dhan had said that it did not surprise him that the Western ideal of basing relationships on romantic love should be doomed to failure. Compatibility and respect were far more important in the long run. And Luke had agreed with him—every word.

Luke watched now as Holly excitedly browsed

through paint charts, impatiently scooping great handfuls of fiery curls away from her pale cheeks.

He wanted her, he thought guiltily. Far too much.

He cleared his throat and spoke to the assistant, who had spent the last ten minutes gazing at him mistily. 'I presume you have professional decorators you recommend?' he asked.

The assistant nodded and fluttered her lashes at him. 'Oh, yes, sir!'

He gave her his lazy smile. 'So how soon could I have a shop decorated?'

The assistant paused. Some people you could fob off. Others you wouldn't want to. Some people came into this shop with their symbols of wealth ostentatiously displayed. This man wore faded jeans and a sheepskin jacket and a pair of desert boots. There was no expensive watch gleaming discreetly on his wrist, and yet he exuded that certain something which spoke of power.

The assistant gave a smile she reserved solely for the really *hunky* customers. 'How soon do you *want* it decorated, sir?' she asked him pertly.

CHAPTER FIVE

'So—' Luke handed Holly a cup of coffee and tried to inject a little enthusiasm into his voice. 'A week to go.'

'And counting.'

They looked at one another in silence over the breakfast table.

'It's been less...problematic having you here than I thought,' Luke said heavily. He had been down to the shop first thing, irritated to discover that for the first time in *his* experience, the building work was actually coming in on *time*!

'Well, it isn't quite over yet,' said Holly.

'No.'

The thought of moving out appalled her; she felt extremely comfortable where she was, thank you very much. And she liked Luke—she liked him a great deal.

Not that she had anything to be miserable about, not really. The business part of her—though still in a very embryonic state—was delighted that all the work on the shop was going according to schedule. It would be wonderful to hang a sign on the door saying 'Open'. To have all those dewy-eyed brides-to-be arriving and flicking through her sample swatches of Thai silk and duchesse satin.

But these past few days in Luke's company...

Holly sighed, recognising that somewhere along the way she had become completely captivated by him.

Whether or not he had intended for it to happen, she
didn't know. She certainly hadn't *intended* to be held in
thrall by those faded denim-blue eyes and the dark hair
kissed with gold…

And when she thought about it logically, it wasn't
really surprising that she was so reluctant to move out.
There couldn't be many women who wouldn't enjoy
sharing a house with a man like Luke Goodwin! A man
with manners, who cooked, who read and who could
make her laugh.

In fact, his only fault—apart from his unfair attraction
to the opposite sex—was a distinct *bossiness*, and the
idea that he was somehow always right.

He gave her a challenging look over the breakfast table. 'Right, Holly,' he said sternly. 'You might as well
get your car looked at. You're not using it much at the
moment. There's a Beetle dealer in Winchester—he can
tell you what it's worth, if you really want to sell it.'

'I can't remember saying that I wanted to sell it,' she
objected.

'Didn't you?' His eyes were baby-blue innocent.
'Well, it's up to you—but think of frosty mornings like
yesterday, when it wouldn't start.'

When the car had glittered like a magnificent red and
yellow jewel—but Holly's breath had been great white
puffs of smoke, and her fingers had ended up blue and
numb. And Luke had actually scowled, and got angry,
and told her she was irresponsible, and asked how she
was intending to cope if it broke down in the middle of
a country lane at the dead of night.

'Okay,' she sighed. 'Let's go and see the car dealer.'

He drove her into the city, where she was quoted a

very healthy price which made her think seriously about selling. And while they were in town she went to see the signwriter whom she had persuaded to decorate the front of the shop in the most unforgettable and spectacular style before Saturday.

It was almost six as they drove along the back roads out of Winchester towards Woodhampton, and Luke glanced over at her in the dim light of the car.

'Fancy stopping off for supper on the way home?'

'I'd love to,' she whispered in delight, then could have kicked herself. How did she manage to come over like a sixteen-year-old being asked out on a first date!

Luke frowned in the semi-darkness. She confused the hell out of him; she blushed, she stumbled, she turned wide green eyes on him which made him feel guilty for wanting her. Which he did. Still. Frequently.

Sometimes she sounded as naive as a schoolgirl. An image which did not tally with the foxy way she had of looking at him sometimes. Or the way she looked herself… Today she was wearing dark velvet trousers which clung sinfully to those long legs of hers as she crossed one slim ankle over another. He tore his eyes away only just in time to narrowly miss bumping over a rock on the side of the road.

'Damn!'

'Don't swear, Luke,' she commented mildly.

Then cover up, he felt like saying, but resisted.

At the pub they settled down to eat plates of curry and half-pints of lager.

'That was good,' said Luke, wiping his mouth with a napkin and pushing the empty plate away. 'Reminds me of Sunday lunches out in Kenya.'

'Does it?' She stared at a piece of poppadom. 'And did you eat *these*?'

He grinned. 'Sometimes.'

'So was life very different out there?'

'Different to what?'

'Well...' she looked around the pub, glittering and gaudy with metallic streamers '...different to this.'

He looked at her. At the way her hair blazed like the sunsets he'd watched while drinking a beer in the hot dust at the end of the day. He thought about it. 'Yeah. Very different. The days are ruled by the seasons and the animals.'

'And was it a very big game reserve?'

He smiled then, a relaxed smile, thinking that she asked questions with the absorption of a child. 'There aren't really any little reserves, Holly! You need a plane to get around. I used to fly my little super-cub over the place—checking the herds and counting the game. Sometimes I'd get up early at six, and take the hot air balloon up—'

'Seriously?'

He smiled. 'Sure. It's the best time of all—very, very beautiful, and the wind is quite still. The animals don't even know you're there, and you can see cheetah kills or check if any damage has been done by the odd rogue elephant. If there were any injured animals I'd go back for them with a vehicle, and bring them back and tend to them.'

'And you loved the animals?' she quizzed softly.

'Not in the way you think.'

'And what way is that?'

'It's not like having a puppy running round the place;

not the same kind of thing at all. Man's relationship with wild animals tends to be based on mutual respect, but they aren't tame and they never will be.'

'So they don't love you unconditionally? I thought that was the thing which motivated people to work with animals.'

He shook his tawny head. 'Nope. If you're lucky, you can earn their trust—and that's a pretty good feeling.'

No wonder he looked so rugged and brown and strong. Holly stared at the strong lines of his jaw and again felt that stupid urge to trace her finger along its proud curve. 'I've never met a real-life adventurer before.'

'Hey!' he contradicted softly, with a shake of his head. 'It's just a job, Holly.'

'Not really,' she mused. 'It's hardly putting on your suit and getting on the 8:05 every morning with a rolled-up umbrella under your arm!' And it seemed such *physical* work, too. Most of the men she'd met in her life wouldn't have been able to punch their way out of a wet paper bag. Somehow she didn't picture Luke having any trouble. 'How about time off? What did you do then?'

He looked at her, imagined the vast African sun gilding her hair. 'Oh, I walked a lot—there are some beautiful rivers out there. Sometimes I camped out under the stars. I grew an orchard of oranges and lemons and had freshly squeezed juice for breakfast. Sometimes I'd get on a horse and just ride.'

'So it was solitary?'

'Sometimes.'

She opened her mouth to ask him about women, but something stopped her and she shut it again. She didn't want to know. Didn't want to lie in bed at night and torture herself—imagining those strong brown limbs tangled with someone other than *her*.

God, what was she *thinking*? She swallowed. That she'd like to go to bed with him—*that* was what she was thinking.

He narrowed his eyes. 'Why, Holly, you look awfully hot under the collar,' he commented on a murmur. 'Why ever's that?'

'Too many layers on,' she mumbled, and took a huge mouthful of lager.

But she might as well have been a nun for all the notice he took of her. In the same situation, any other man might have leapt on her, but, while only a fool would deny that *something* fizzled through the air between them, Luke behaved like a perfect gentleman. Holly felt protected and safe; safer than she could ever remember.

Just my luck, she thought gloomily that night, as she lay in bed reading what the competition was up to in *English Brides*. You find a man you can spin wild fantasies about and he treats you like a maiden aunt!

Still, at least there was plenty of work to keep herself occupied, while Luke sat in the study, frowning like mad over his legal documents, or driving out to a farm his uncle had owned on the edge of the county which he said was driving him nuts because no money had been invested in it for years.

'It will need a total rethink,' he prophesied grimly, pleased that he had managed to offload Doug Reasdale without too much unpleasantness.

'And is that what you're going to do in England?' asked Holly tentatively. 'Build on your inheritance?'

'I guess,' he mused. 'Maybe I'll make a fortune and then give it all away to someone who needs it more than me.'

There weren't *many* people who could have said that and made it believable, thought Holly—but Luke was one of them.

She had her dress samples sent down from London, and Luke gave her the use of a large ground-floor room to hang the wedding gowns up in. When they arrived she spent most of the day ironing them, and he brought her in a cup of coffee just as she was steaming the creases out of a silver taffeta gown with a huge skirt and a silver bodice encrusted with beads.

He stood looking at the elaborate creation for a moment, then frowned. 'Do you like that?' he asked her doubtfully.

Holly hid a smile. 'This? It isn't my particular favourite,' she admitted.

'Looks a bit like one of those dolls that some people use to cover up loo rolls,' he observed.

'They don't generally use pure silk-taffeta for those!' she laughed. She sat back on her heels to look up at him, then wished she hadn't. From here, it was all too easy to start fantasising about those endless legs...

She began to chatter brightly instead. 'This is a more traditional dress, because brides often come shopping with their mothers. And, no matter how way-out the bride might be, mothers do tend to like traditional dresses!'

'Do they?' he questioned thoughtfully. His eyes flicked over the other dresses on the rail. 'I'm surprised that hardly any of them are white—I thought that's what brides wore.'

It occurred to Holly that this was a man who knew very little about weddings. 'Brides have worn different colours throughout the ages—but, yes, you're right, white was the predominant colour for many years.'

'But not any more?'

'That's right.'

'Now they wear cream?'

'Ivory,' she corrected. 'Which suits most people's skin tones much better. White can be a difficult colour to carry off.'

'And its associations are obsolete?' he suggested drawlingly.

Holly looked at him. 'Meaning?'

Luke shrugged. 'Well, white is traditionally the colour of virgins, and most brides these days are no longer virgins. Are they?'

Afraid that she would start stuttering like a starter gun, Holly put the steamer down, took the coffee from him and carried it over to the window. 'Er, no. They're not.' It was time to change the subject. She really didn't feel up to discussing the modern decline of bridal virginity— not with Luke, anyway.

She realised that not once had he mentioned his own family—bar his uncle, who had left him this house, and that had been only fleetingly. He was an enigmatic man, that was the trouble. He kept his cards very close to his chest, and of course that made him all the more intriguing. Holly was so used to meeting men who told you their entire life story within the first five minutes of meeting them that she wasn't sure how to cope with a man who kept his own counsel!

She stood savouring the bitter, strong aroma of the coffee for a moment, before plucking up the courage to say, 'Are either of your parents still alive, Luke?'

'No,' he answered shortly.

She took another sip of her coffee, recognising that a barrier had come slamming down. Fair enough. Her own life had been unconventional and she knew that people prying only made her hackles rise in defence. She smiled at him instead. 'You know, you're absolutely right—you *do* make the best coffee in the world!'

Luke's mouth softened. So she wasn't overly inquisitive. The fact that she had correctly picked up the signals and retreated made him far less inclined to clam up about his past. And friendship was a two-way game— she'd told him plenty about herself. 'My mother was an opera singer,' he told her, going to stand beside her by the window.

It was not what she had imagined, not in a million years. She let out a low whistle. 'I'm impressed!'

But he shook his head as he stared into the middle distance. 'Don't be. She wasn't a soloist, more a jobbing singer. So she had all of the sacrifice and insecurity with none of the glory.' His smile held a sideways tilt of resignation. 'But still she carried on singing.'

'She must have loved it very much to continue,' commented Holly.

'Oh, there was ego involved, and certainly passion,' he commented wryly. 'Which are the two main motivating forces behind the arts.'

'Ego and passion? Hmm! Yet *another* generalisation from Mr Goodwin!' laughed Holly.

'Maybe,' he shrugged. 'But I think that artists generally have a better time than their unfortunate offspring.'

'You mean that they don't make good parents?' she asked tentatively, aware that the answer was suddenly terribly important to her. Because he thought of *her* as an artist? And if he damned their parenting skills in general, then surely he would also be damning her?

'I don't think they do make good parents, no. Try explaining to a five-year-old why Mummy has to go off for months on end on tour.' He shot her a swift look. 'Why the adulation of an audience means more than that of your small child.'

She glanced up at him. 'And did you have a father anywhere on the scene?'

'Oh, yes.' He watched the steam rise from his coffee. 'He used to care for me during my mother's absences, even turning a blind eye to her little dalliances.'

Holly's eyes widened. 'You mean she had...'

'Affairs?' he supplied acidly. 'I most certainly do. If there was one thing my beautiful, artistic mother excelled at, it was having affairs.'

'Heavens,' commented Holly uncertainly.

'They were necessary to that ego of hers again—to show that she was still a desirable woman.'

'I see.' The bitter disapproval in his voice was unmistakable and understandable. Holly put down her empty cup on the window sill and turned to face him. 'What happened to them? Your parents, I mean?'

There was a pause. His words were like lemon pips.

'My mother died of an infection abroad, when I was eight—'

'Oh, *Luke*,' said Holly, her heart going out to him. 'What a terrible thing to happen.'

He was caught in the sympathetic light from her eyes, and something in that emerald blaze started an aching deep within him, but he quashed it as ruthlessly as he would a fly. 'Yeah,' he agreed quietly, that one small word telling her more than anything just how bad it must have been.

She wanted to go and hug him, to take him tightly in her arms and enfold him, to soothe all that little-boy hurt away.

He saw the way she was looking at him, and it made him want to lose himself in the velvet softness of her lips, to melt and meld into the shuddering sweetness of her body. But he shook his head in denial, trying to get a handle on his senses.

'It *was* a terrible thing to happen,' he said quite calmly, as though these were words he had repeated many times. 'My father never really got over it. He loved her, you see—for all her capriciousness and her fickleness, her inability to accept reality. When she died it was as though a light had gone off inside him—'

'He gave up, you mean?'

'Not in the physical sense. He continued to care for me as best he could. A housekeeper cooked my meals and cleaned my clothes, and my father gave me what love he was capable of. Summer holidays were the worst—we lived in London, and the city used to feel like a cage during those long weeks. His brother began inviting me down here during the vacations—and the sense of freedom and space was a real eye-opener.'

Holly stared out of the window again, at the bare-branched beauty of the winter landscape. She imagined those same trees clothed in green, the summer flowers bursting into rainbow radiance. Yes, she thought, this place must have seemed like a paradise to a motherless little city boy. She turned back to him, her eyes full of questions. 'And?'

Luke looked at her with interest. Most people had usually overdosed on sadness by this stage in his story. Not that he had told it for a long time. Even Caroline had blithely told him that bad memories were best pushed away and forgotten. That cans of worms were best left unopened. He found himself wondering fleetingly whether she was right.

'My father died just after I finished school. It was as though he had been hanging on until he had seen through his parental responsibility. I was lined up to go to university—it was something my father wanted badly for me. Then, when he died, I suddenly thought, I don't have to *do* this any more—in fact, I don't have to do *anything* I don't want any more.'

'And that's when you went out to Africa?' Holly guessed. 'For even more of the space you had come to love here? And to escape the unhappy associations with England. And the past.'

'Intuitive of you,' he observed.

'It's one of the more positive sides of being artistic,' she told him archly. 'It isn't all *ego*, you know!'

'Did I offend you with my comments?' he drawled, noticing that she had failed to mention passion.

'The truth never offends me.' She was aware of him watching her closely. Too closely. Her long-limbed body seemed to suddenly lack co-ordination; her hand was shaking as she picked up the steamer once more and moved back towards the silver gown. 'I guess I'd better get back to work.'

'Yes.' But he remained rooted to the spot, transfixed by the sight of her. Today she was dressed in some filmy-looking skirt covered in a delicate floral print, which flowed all the way down to her slender ankles. The shirt she wore was white and loose and gauzy, and she had some sort of dark, tight vest beneath it, so it certainly wasn't indecent. But there was something about a woman in a diaphanous piece of clothing which would make any hot-blooded male's heart pound.

And Luke's was pounding now.

He swallowed, trying to ease the hot dryness in his mouth, the ache between his legs. He needed to get out of here. Away from here. Fast.

'I'm going out,' he told her abruptly.

'Oh?' said Holly pleasantly. 'Going somewhere nice?' she heard herself asking, as if she were his form teacher!

'Just out.' Damn her, and her curiosity. He had offered her house room for a couple of weeks and suddenly she was his keeper? 'I'll see you later,' he said tersely, and took himself off to telephone Caroline.

'Sure,' agreed Holly, in a casual tone which didn't quite come off. His abruptness hurt. Was he angry with himself for giving away too much? For opening up a heart she suspected had been ramparted for too many years? She picked up a needle and began to sew, and presently the comforting rhythm of the needle and thread made her feel calm once more.

Holly spent the next couple of days checking she had done everything that her guidebook to starting a new business told her to. She knew how important it was for her to establish strong links with all the other local companies associated with weddings. She needed to get to know caterers and car-hire companies, the managers of popular wedding venues and local florists. That way, they all helped one another.

She took her car into Winchester and discovered that the best florist in the city was the one who had been displaying the holly wreath which had caught Luke's eye that day when they'd braved the Christmas shoppers together.

The assistant who had ogled Luke so appreciatively went out to the back room to find the shop's owner, and Michelle McCormack appeared almost immediately.

She was a tiny dynamo of a woman, aged around thirty, with eyes the colour of expensive chocolate and glossy brown hair which was tied back in a dark green ribbon to match the green pinafore she wore. She was imaginative and enthusiastic, and she and Holly hit it off straight away. They went into the back of the shop to browse over the big book of wedding bouquets over cups of tea.

'I need plenty of fresh flowers for the opening on Saturday,' Holly explained as she peered at a photo which featured a stunning combination of cornflowers and sunflowers. 'For decorating the shop window—

that's as well as bouquets for the window. But naturally, this volume of blooms is a one-off.'

'After that, I could supply a mixture of silk flowers and fresh?' suggested Michelle. 'Fresh flowers should be saved for special occasions, because they don't last long and it won't set your beautiful dresses off if you have wilting petals in the shop window! Some occasions would obviously need fresh posies for the window.'

Holly nodded. 'All the key festivals, really. Brides get ideas at holiday times.'

'White lilies at Easter,' said Michelle dreamily. 'And scarlet silk peonies for Valentine's. Can I clash colours and break rules?'

'As long as you make them as well!' giggled Holly as she saw her dream begin to gather real substance. 'I want you to be as creative as I intend to be!'

Michelle gave Holly a penetrating stare just before she left, and said, 'So where's your hunk?'

It would have been pointless and rather pathetic to have expressed ignorance of whom she was talking about. Holly shrugged. 'Luke? I don't know—and anyway, he isn't *my* hunk.'

Michelle licked her lips exaggeratedly. 'Then can *I* have him, please?'

'You haven't even seen him!' protested Holly.

'No, but my assistant has—and I value her judgement on most things! Just tell me one thing—has she been exaggerating about his extraordinary beauty and sex appeal?'

Holly couldn't lie. 'Er, no,' she confessed. 'She hasn't.'

After seeing Michelle, Holly went in person to talk to

a reporter from the *Winchester Echo*, guessing that she would get better coverage if she laid on the charm offensive in person, rather than just telephoning.

The cub reporter was called Pete, and he was young and enthusiastic.

Holly gave him all the details while he scribbled them down.

'And you say you won a competition?'

'That's right. Sponsored by *Beautiful Brides*.'

'And the cheque was sufficient to get you started up in business?'

'Only just!'

'Interesting story,' he mused. He wrote something else down, then looked up. 'And where's this dress now? The winning design?'

'I have it packed away,' she told him. 'It's being featured in next March's issue of *Beautiful Brides*. I shall be unveiling it—if you'll excuse the pun!—on Saturday at the opening, and every person who visits the shop during the month of December will be entered into a draw to win the dress!'

Pete pursed his lips together and made a clicking sound with his teeth. 'Good publicity stunt,' he breathed, then smiled at her as he flicked his notebook shut and stood up. 'And it'll make a brilliant story!'

'I certainly hope so.'

'See you Saturday, then!'

On the way home, Holly couldn't resist going to peep at the shop, which was a flurry of activity. People were sawing wood and painting and knocking nails in walls. From the direction of the upstairs flat came the sound of a drill being used. She parked the car, and was standing outside for a moment, unsure of whether or not to go right inside, when a familiar figure came striding out of the shop, and predictably her heart leapt like a salmon.

He was dressed in a pair of faded jeans which matched his eyes and a fleecy blue-check shirt which made them look even bluer. His gold-tipped hair was sprinkled with sawdust that made Holly think of fairy dust, but his eyes were wary and reminded her that he'd been keeping his distance lately.

'Hello, Holly,' he said carefully. 'I thought you were going to stay away until everything was ready?'

'You sound as though you're warning me off!' she told him crossly.

Or himself, Luke thought grimly, before forcing a smile to hide behind. 'Well, I'd hardly do that, would I?' He forced his voice to sound placatory, but it wasn't easy. He had two more days of this to endure—just two more days and then his life would be Holly-free. He would be able to sleep nights. Eat a meal without having lustful thoughts about the morsels disappearing into that pink and delectable mouth of hers. He couldn't wait. 'When it's your shop.'

'*Your* shop, you mean,' she corrected sulkily, as she recalled her conversation with Michelle McCormack. He was the kind of man who made total strangers want to chat him up—so what chance did *she* have? Quite apart from the fact that his moods were so mercurial. One minute he seemed like her best buddy, while the next...

'If it's my shop then you have certainly made your mark on it,' he commented drily. 'Since I hadn't planned on green, gold and purple walls—or a bleached wood floor!'

Holly made herself sound grateful, and she *was* grateful. After all, there couldn't be many landlords who would decorate a shop exactly to the new leaseholder's specifications. If only he wouldn't be so spiky! 'It's lovely,' she said obediently, and pressed her nose up against the window.

'Well, it's not finished yet.' He looked down at her with a curious frown. 'What's up? I thought you'd be a lot more excited than this.'

'Oh.' Holly shrugged as she searched around for something to say. Something suitable. Rather than something along the lines of, I'm going to miss you, Luke Goodwin. I'm going to miss seeing that lazy smile which you give out so rarely, but when you do it's like the sun blinding you with its radiant power. 'I guess that the realisation of just what I've taken on has finally hit me.'

'Can't cope, huh?' he teased.

She slitted her eyes at him like a cat. 'Just watch me!'

He turned away—he had to, for fear that she would see him harden in front of her eyes. For God's sake— what was the matter with him? Getting erections like a schoolboy? It was sheer bloody instinct, this response. And a sheer bloody inconvenience, too. His voice was gritty as he spoke over his shoulder. 'Are you going back up to the house?'

'No, Luke—I'm planning to make myself a comfy bed of sawdust and sleep right here!'

He turned then, exasperation and humour making his mouth twist and curve in all directions. 'Any idea what you'd like to eat later?' Evenings were becoming increasingly difficult, but he found that he could cope with her a little better if they weren't on mutual territory.

Squashy sofas and large, comfortable beds within carrying distance were proving something of a distraction. 'We could always go to that pub again. Or find a restaurant, maybe?'

But Holly was reluctant. If they went out as a couple, it only served to remind her that they *weren't* actually a couple, much as she would have liked them to be. She shook her head. 'I'll probably just have some eggs and an early night. I've still got lots of paperwork to do—figures that need going over.'

'Everything adding up okay?'

She knew he found it fascinating that she could tot up a column of figures in her head. 'Just because I majored in art doesn't mean I'm a complete dough-brain when it comes to sums, you know!'

'I know! I know! Skip the lecture, Holly. I think you're brilliant in almost every way!'

'Almost?'

'If only you could cook!' he sighed, and gestured behind him with his thumb. 'Better get back in there—it's been years since I did any carpentry!'

Holly walked through the already dark village street towards the silhouetted arch of the yew bush which framed his beautiful house. Then she stood still for a moment, and just stared.

Saturday would be the first of December and the opening of her brand-new shop. She was an adult, a grown-up—on the start of something big. Something exciting.

Why, then, did the thought of Saturday and leaving Luke make her feel as miserable as when the tooth fairy forgot to visit?

CHAPTER SIX

AN OLD-FASHIONED bell chimed out as Luke pushed open the shop door and stepped inside.

Perched halfway up a stepladder, Holly halted in the middle of hanging a bunch of golden balloons from the ceiling and looked down expectantly at him. It was important to her what he thought. Everything about the day so far had been good—it was crisp and clear, with golden sunshine gilding the intense blue of the early December sky. And all the work had been finished bang on time.

Outside, painted in old gold on a deep green background, the shop sign bore the legend 'Lovelace Brides'. In the window itself, a faceless mannequin wore Holly's prize-winning dress. The ivory duchesse satin gleamed with all the milky lustre of moonlight, the soft, heavy material falling in perfect folds from the pleated waist. The stark simplicity of the style simply took the breath away. Or so the departing builders had told a pleased and bemused Holly—though she didn't have them marked down as wedding dress experts!

The mannequin was holding an exquisite bouquet designed by Michelle—a winter bouquet bright with glossy green foliage and scarlet berries, waxy white Christmas roses and sprigs of mistletoe.

In the background a CD played bridal music to add to the mood—at the moment it was trumpeting out the awesome majesty of 'Pomp and Circumstance'. And, all in all, Holly felt that there was little she could do to improve anything in the shop.

But Luke's opinion was somehow as important to Holly as all the other component parts which went to make up a success. He had put himself out on a limb by letting her choose the colour scheme, he had trusted her judgement—and she desperately wanted him to like it.

Luke looked around and took it all in very, very slowly. With the deep, rich colours she had chosen the effect could have been claustrophobic, but the high ceilings and elegant proportions of the building meant that it was exactly the opposite. Peacock, golden and purple. It was both ancient and modern—ageless and timeless. The huge mirrors on each wall which were a necessary feature of all bridal shops—since every angle of the bride had to be seen and scrutinised—reflected the colours and the space back and back again.

'Well, well, well,' said Luke, very softly.

'Do you like it?' she asked him quietly as she climbed down off the ladder and stood in front of him.

'I like it very much,' he replied. 'How about you?'

'I love it.'

'You left very early this morning.' He narrowed his eyes at her in question. 'With all your gear.'

'Well, I had a lot to do. And you were sleeping.'

'Oh?' There was a hint of teasing humour in the blue glint of his eyes. 'Did you come in and check up on me, then, Holly?'

'I—stuck my head round the door.' Holly picked up a silver balloon and began to tie it to another, wondering whether he would notice that her fingers were trembling with the memory.

It had been a daunting and magnificent sight—Luke's bronzed and muscular body sprawled carelessly out over most of a double bed. He had been covered by a duvet, true, but some of his chest had been bare and Holly's eye had been drawn with fascination to the riot of gold-tipped hair which grew there. The soft feathers of the goose down quilt had moulded themselves closely to his shape—defining each muscular leg as it shifted rest-lessly, causing Holly to leave the room more hurriedly than she had intended.

'Well, I didn't hear you,' he observed softly. He al-ways slept in the raw, and now he found that his pulses were leaping with unbearable excitement at the thought of Holly watching him while he lay sleeping. 'You should have woken me.'

She had been tempted—oh, yes! For one brief, mad moment of fantasy she had actually contemplated step-ping out of her warm and cosy pyjamas and climbing in naked beside him, wrapping her soft skin against the hardened contours of his body. In the fantasy which fol-lowed he said nothing, just pulled her into his arms and began to kiss her very thoroughly. And that was as far as she had got before fleeing the room as sanity had seeped back in.

Luke walked up and down the shop, past the flowing silks and satins of the dress rail full of samples. He paused for a moment beside the pale frothy haze of bri-dal veils, with their pearled or glittery tiaras. There were shoes too, in different styles, lined up in neat lines, like rows of ivory satin soldiers. While right in the corner lay tiny drifts of minuscule bras and panties in finest silks and Belgian lace.

'*Underwear?*' he asked her, in surprise.

Holly flushed a horrid, unbecoming shade of magenta. 'There's no need to look so shocked!' she complained.

He shook his head, the corners of his mouth lifting with amusement. 'I'm not shocked,' he told her. 'Merely curious. Fascinated, actually—as to why you're flogging knickers in a bridal shop!'

Holly sighed. 'You men can be so dense sometimes! Because the bride-to-be is under enough stress as it is. What she wants is to *simplify* her life—and you can do that by saving her time. You sell as much as possible of what she wants to wear on the big day under one roof. And bridal underwear is a little bit specialised.'

'Oh?'

'It must be the very best—the finest silks, the purest lace—'

'The flimsiest?' he suggested with an ironic smile, as he impudently dangled a cream lace tanga from his index finger.

Holly's eyes swam as the image of him holding the wisp of lace imprinted itself onto her mind. It looked— and she felt her heart race like fury—looked as if he had just slid that outrageous little garment off. Off *her*, perhaps? Oh-oh! There was that lethal wishful thinking again! She couldn't look him in the face, let alone the eye, so instead she bent to pick up an imaginary speck of dust from the softly gleaming floorboards.

'The house seems very bare without you,' he said suddenly.

Holly swallowed down the lump of emotion which

had risen in her throat and aimed for humour. 'And very quiet, I imagine?'

Dark eyebrows were elevated. 'Well, there *is* that,' he admitted, with a smile.

He stood looking at her; he could have stood there looking at her all day. 'You look fantastic, Holly,' he said.

'Do I?' Holly searched helplessly for another speck of dust. She was wearing a daring thigh-high tunic made of thin layers of embroidered cream voile, with sheer floaty sleeves gathered tightly at the wrist. It was one of her own designs, which was what people would expect, and could *almost* be a wedding dress—if the bride had absolutely no qualms about showing acres of leg! 'Honestly?'

'Honestly. I didn't realise you had legs.' He let his eyes linger on them. Bad mistake. Luke quelled the heat which was threatening to rise.

'You, um...you look very...very nice yourself,' said Holly tamely, because she thought that 'sensational' might be a little too strong an adjective! She wasn't used to seeing him dressed up—in fact, she realised that this was the first time she had seen him in anything other than faded denims.

He usually looked much more like a ranch hand than a man of some means, but today was the closest he had got to that particular image, in a shirt of delphinium silk and dark navy trousers. Yet he didn't look a bit like a stuffed shirt, which a lot of men did if they weren't used to wearing smart clothes. Luke just looked sexy. Unbelievably sexy. 'Very nice,' she finished.

'Why, thank you,' he answered drily, but he found that he was absurdly flattered by her halting compliment.

The darkening of his eyes was immensely flattering, but Holly found that it was making her feel light-headed, and she couldn't think straight. Her voice sounded faint. 'I-I'd better go and open some wine.'

'I'll do it.' He followed her out to the small, newly fitted kitchen at the back of the shop and took the corkscrew she handed him. 'What time are they arriving?'

'Soon.' But not soon enough, thought Holly with a swift glance at her watch. Much more time alone with Luke and she would surely do something unforgivable, like hurling herself into his arms and asking him to kiss her. Every bit of her!

She tipped crisps and peanuts into bowls and lined up the glasses she had hired for the day, while Luke extracted corks from wine bottles like an expert. They worked together in companionable silence, and Holly wasn't sure whether to be pleased or not when she heard the clanging of the doorbell as the first of her invited guests arrived.

It was Michelle McCormack, the florist. She was dressed in apple-green and had brought two girlfriends with her. 'Candy and Mary are both getting married in the summer,' she told Holly excitedly. 'So they're going to be your first two customers!'

'Please don't feel under any pressure,' Holly told them, with a smile.

'Now that's not the right marketing approach!' scolded Michelle, but Holly shook her head.

'On the contrary—I'm confident that with one look— they'll be hooked!'

'Well, why don't we put it to the test?' suggested Candy with a giggle, and she and Mary went off to gaze longingly at the wedding dresses.

'Who'd like some wine?' asked a deep voice behind them, and Holly watched as Michelle turned round and was momentarily transfixed by the sight of Luke Goodwin, resplendent in the soft silk shirt, his blue eyes glittering like a sun-kissed sea.

'Me, too,' whispered Michelle, goggle-eyed.

'Me, too—what?' asked Holly, blinking with confusion.

'One look and *I'm* hooked!'

From Luke's faint smile, Holly guessed that he must have heard, but Michelle didn't appear to mind—or maybe it had been her intention that he heard!

Holly introduced them. 'Luke, this is Michelle McCormack, who is responsible for all the beautiful flowers you can see. Michelle, this is Luke Goodwin— he owns the shop.'

'You *own* it?' Michelle's eyes widened into saucers as she took a glass of white wine from him. 'Holly didn't tell me you were rich as well as beautiful!'

'I don't remember saying he was beautiful, either!' said Holly crossly.

'Didn't you?' queried Luke, with a teasing smile. 'Oh, Holly—now I *am* disappointed!'

'Why don't we find a quiet corner together, Luke?' suggested Michelle. 'And then you can tell me your life story.'

Luke smiled. Women like Michelle he could cope with. Charming. Flirtatious. A bit over-the-top, maybe. But ultimately safe. There were no secrets or mysteries lurking behind Michelle McComack's dark eyes. What you saw was what you got. 'Love to,' he replied easily.

Holly tried not to feel indignant or jealous or miffed—not when she knew that she had no right to feel anything other than gratitude towards Luke. Thanks to him, she had a shop which would not have looked out of place in one of London's most exclusive streets.

The bell rang once more and the place began to fill up. Holly had sent an invitation to the local vicar, and, much to her astonishment, he turned up on a motorbike! He had collar-length blond hair, a face of almost cherubic innocence, and looked far too young to be legally entrusted with the task of performing marriages!

'Hi, Holly, I'm Charles Cape,' he told her, and held out his hand. 'Pleased to meet you.'

'Thanks for coming,' smiled Holly, who had thought he would toss the invitation into the nearest bin.

But he shook his head. 'No—thanks for inviting me.' He grinned. 'Don't look so surprised that I'm here! Apart from wanting to meet you, since you're new to the village, we're both in the business of making marriage more attractive to the general public, aren't we?'

'I suppose we are,' she agreed thoughtfully.

Holly changed the music to an old-fashioned Christmas tape and began to refill everyone's glasses, and soon the shop took on a party-like atmosphere, particularly when a few people plucked up courage and began to walk in off the street.

'*She* doesn't look like she's in the market for a wedding dress!' whispered one of Michelle's friends to Holly, as a well-padded woman of about eighty plonked herself down on one of the window seats and began to glug contentedly at a glass of wine.

'No, but she might have granddaughters who will be,' said Holly, as she moved a bowl of peanuts away from the satin shoes.

Pete Thomas, the reporter from the *Winchester Echo*, had turned up with a photographer in tow.

'We want to emphasise the wedding dress competition,' he told Holly. 'It's a good angle—and it's different. When are you planning to make the draw?'

'On January the First,' said Holly. 'First day of the New Year. New beginnings, and all that. We won't be open—but I'll announce the winner in the window.' She glanced across the room to where Luke was still sitting, chatting to Michelle, only they had now been joined by Michelle's two friends.

For two brides-to-be, they were certainly paying a lot of interest to whatever Luke was saying, were Holly's rather caustic thoughts. But she ignored the nagging feeling of jealousy and went round, topping everyone's glasses up, until the shop was buzzing with chatter.

People began to filter away just before three, when some of the light had already begun to fade from the sky.

Michelle stood up to go, swayed on her high heels and giggled as she put her hand onto Luke's shoulder to steady herself.

'Whoops! Too much wine on an empty stomach. I need sustenance! How about you, Luke? A big, strong man like you could probably do with a plate of food, right?'

He shrugged and gave a regretful smile. 'Perhaps

some other time. I promised Holly I'd help her tidy away,' he demurred smoothly, meeting a pair of pleased but bewildered emerald eyes over Michelle's head.

Michelle shot Holly another envious look. 'A boss who tidies up? Where have I been going wrong for all these years?' She smiled. 'Well, you know where I am, Luke. If you're ever in Winchester and you fancy some company.'

'I'll be sure to bear that in mind.' He smiled again.

Holly stood at the door, saying goodbye to those who were leaving, though part of her was distracted, wondering whether women came on to Luke like that on a regular basis. He must have an address book like an encyclopedia, she found herself thinking wistfully. No wonder he never talked about women—he'd probably lost count!

'Bye, darling!' trilled Michelle, giving Holly the benefit of a rather glassy smile.

'They loved your flowers,' Holly told her softly.

'I loved your boss,' retorted Michelle. 'Is he free, do you know?'

Holly resisted the urge to tell her no—that if Luke Goodwin was lined up for anyone, then it was her. But that would be the act of a child, not a woman. She nodded, and copper ringlets dangled around her face like burnished corkscrews as she quickly turned her head to check that he wasn't listening. 'Well, he hasn't talked about a particular woman since I've been here—and he's definitely not married—so I think it's fairly safe to say he isn't in love.'

'So he's all mine?' Michelle queried, with a delighted grin.

'Well...' Holly smiled as Michelle planted a wine-laden kiss of farewell on her cheek. 'That's rather up to him, isn't it?'

'Mmm,' said Michelle. 'I'm metaphorically licking my lips at the thought of it!'

Everyone bar Luke had left by four, by which time the faint silver blink of stars had begun to pepper the indigo sky.

Holly looked around. What had happened to her beautiful shop? On every available surface were empty and half-empty wine glasses, bowls containing the remaining crumbs of crisps and peanuts, and lying on the wooden floor were two fading white roses which someone had obviously plucked out of one of Michelle's flower arrangements.

'Why the sour face?' came a deep voice from behind her. 'I thought it went very well.'

'It did. It went brilliantly.' She drew a breath, then flapped her hands around. 'It's just that it all looks such a mess!'

He threw her a disbelieving look. 'Can this be the same woman who, days ago, was about to inhabit a building which resembled a corporation tip?'

'Yes, I was. But that's the whole point,' she argued firmly. 'Once a place looks beautiful, you want to try like mad to keep it that way.'

He walked towards the kitchen at the back.

'Where are you going?' asked Holly curiously.

'To find a tray for the empty glasses. Come on—I'll help you clear up.'

CHAPTER SEVEN

LUKE washed all the glasses and dishes while Holly re-arranged flowers, shoes and dresses, and by six the shop was looking pristine once more.

'Now watch this,' said Holly, switching off the main light and pointing to her window display. She had dressed the window to dazzle both during the day and by night, and the effect was exactly what she had been aiming for.

A single spotlight illuminated the prize-winning gown, turning the heavy satin into a buttery gold, while the moonlight added a contrasting silvery sheen all of its own.

For a moment he was silent. 'It's absolutely spectacular,' he told her quietly, and Holly's heart leapt with pleasure as she heard his unequivocal praise. 'Quite stunning.'

'Would you...?' Her words disappeared into the air; she was terrified he would misinterpret them.

In the shadowy half-light his gaze was quizzical. 'Would I what?'

The words spilled out like grain from a sack. 'Would you like to come upstairs and see what they've done to the flat?'

He didn't hesitate, even though the voice of his conscience, the voice of his sanity, told him that he should have done. 'Love to,' he answered.

'After all—you were the one who paid for its decoration!' She wondered why she was tripping over herself to justify the invitation, which was pretty ridiculous when you thought about it. After all, she had shared his house without incident—she was hardly inviting him upstairs in order to start leaping on him!

Luke saw that she was trembling, and frowned. 'Have you had anything to drink?'

She shook her head. 'No, not even a sip. I wanted to keep a clear head, and I was so busy filling up everybody *else's* glasses that I wouldn't have had time to drink my own with any degree of enjoyment!'

'Then how about we open some champagne? To celebrate properly?'

'That would be lovely—but there isn't any, I'm afraid. My budget didn't run to champagne, but perhaps the off-licence might be open?'

Luke laughed, went into the kitchen, and returned—carrying a frosted, foil-topped bottle. 'No, but this very soon will be!' He saw her look of bafflement. 'I brought it with me when I arrived,' he told her softly. 'Didn't you notice? No. Come to think of it, you were too excited to notice anything—'

Not quite true, thought Holly guiltily. She had noticed how wonderful he looked.

'So why don't you take me upstairs now?'

Holly was glad of the half-light, grateful that it would provide some camouflage for the mass of confusions which must have flitted across her face. When he said things like that, he could sound very provocative... She grabbed two glasses and a spare bag of peanuts.

'Come—this way,' she said unsteadily, and the blood pounded like thunder to all her pulse-points.

Upstairs, too, Luke had given her the complete freedom to decorate the flat in the colours of her choice. The leaks were no more, and there was fresh plaster on the ceilings. Luke followed her from room to room and Holly noticed how clean everything smelt—of fresh paint and new wood.

The sitting room was painted a sunny yellow, graduating into deep tangerine in the kitchen. By contrast, the bedroom was blue, although Holly didn't linger there and she noticed that Luke stuck his head round the door only briefly. The tiny bathroom was made to look double its size by the judicious use of mirrors on every wall and Holly was particularly proud of it.

Luke made all the right murmuring sounds of approval, then opened the champagne, and they drank it in the sitting room, in front of the coal-effect gas fire, whose flames flickered convincingly up the chimney.

Sitting on the rug opposite him, Holly drank half a glass of champagne, feeling the alcohol take effect almost immediately, her limbs starting to unfurl as the tensions of the day slowly seeped out of her body.

Luke watched her obsessively, though he was doing his best not to, and wondered just why he had allowed a situation such as the one he now found himself in to develop. Was he merely being protective towards her? Or was he arrogant enough to imagine himself immune to that colt-like beauty of hers?

Holly felt that she ought to say something formal. Something which would remind her that, however kind he was, and however friendly, he remained her landlord—and that he had never shown the remotest sign of wishing to change that relationship. And from today that relationship would change irrevocably, whether she wanted it to or not. Because she would no longer be living with him and that would automatically create a distance between them.

She cleared her throat. 'Thank you for everything you've done for me, Luke. I mean that. Today was a big success—I *hope*!—and I could never have pulled it off if I'd had to handle everything on my own. I probably wouldn't have opened until late summer—and spent most of my capital beforehand. So thanks.'

'It was my pleasure—and I mean *that*.' There was a pause while he considered the wisdom of his next words, but something more powerful than reason made him say them anyway. 'I'm going to miss you, Holly.'

'Will you?' She turned to him with pleasure and surprise.

'Of course I will. You're very good company.'

Holly gave a slightly woozy smile. 'So are you. And I'll miss you, too.'

'Do you suppose we're what's known as a mutual admiration society?' He laughed, and his blue eyes crinkled at the corners.

'I suppose we are,' said Holly breathlessly. He was looking at her in a way that made her heart patter erratically, her skin prickle with heat and excitement. It was as though her body had shifted into a gear she didn't recognise.

He lifted up the bottle. 'Here—have some more champagne.'

'Do you really think I should?'

'Oh, I really do,' he teased, remorselessly slamming the door shut on his doubts.

'Okay, then.' She held her glass out languidly while he topped it up in a cascade of creamy foam, shifting her legs comfortably as she sipped it. Though the oddest thing about champagne was that the more you drank, the thirstier you got. Holly put her head back and sighed dreamily. Everything was too good to be true. Her shop was going to be a success—she just *knew* it was—and sitting opposite her was the most gorgeous man she had ever met. She was floating on a sea of happiness and champagne bubbles.

Luke wished that she wouldn't sit like that. Well, part of him did. The other part of him wanted to replay every movement she had made in slow motion. The tiny cream overskirt had ridden right the way up her legs, and it was proving an extremely distracting sight. He cast around for a safe topic, something which would lead his thoughts away from the milky-white heaven of her thighs. 'So does this feel like home yet?' he asked.

The words were blurted out before she could stop them. 'It does with you here.'

Luke's eyes glinted dangerously. Wasn't she aware that when she said something as silkily as that, with those big green eyes widening up at him like a cat's, he wanted to capture that rosebud mouth of hers and to spend the rest of the night kissing it?

Go, said a voice in his head. Go, now. Before something happens. Before it's too late.

But, for the first time since his teens, desire took precedence over wisdom. His throat felt as though it had been constricted by a vice. Every word a victory. 'Oh?' he asked unsteadily.

Holly shrugged, drained her glass and put it down on the fireplace. 'I've kind of got used to having you around, I suppose. And these last few days…' She hesitated, aware that, if she was totally honest with him, she might come over as weak. And pathetic.

'These last few days….what?' he prompted.

'Well, they've been easy. Relaxed. Civilised.'

'Civilised?' he laughed.

'Sure.' She nodded passionately, too tempted by the clear blue light in his eyes not to lay her feelings bare. 'When I was a student I lived in houses which were too cold and too crowded, and when I was a child I lived in lots of different houses. Houses where I was a stranger— tolerated simply because whoever owned the house really only wanted my mother. I never felt I fitted in—not anywhere. I used to have dreams about proper houses with proper fires, where people made proper meals and ate them sitting at proper tables. Storybook houses that I never really believed in. Except…' and her voice went very quiet '…that yours was exactly like that.'

There was silence while he thought about the import of what she had just told him. Did she not realise just how potent was the power of her vulnerability? The enormous compliment she had just paid him? She was an enigma—with the face and the body of a sorceress and the trusting vulnerability of a little girl. So which was the real Holly Lovelace?

Had he been weak to come up here, or merely foolish? Luke wondered if she could see the tussle on his face. Wondered whether she was deliberately tucking her legs up beneath her like that, so that the movement not only emphasised their length, but also drew attention to the pert thrust of her breasts. His hands felt shaky, his mouth as dry as tinder and, all the while, there was the slow, painful build-up of desire.

He diverted his thoughts by focussing on her words instead of her body. 'Then yours is an upbringing I can identify with,' he told her. 'Only mine was the more institutionalised version of solitary confinement.'

Her hand stilled over the peanuts. 'Tell me.'

The women he had known had not wanted to hear sad stories about dispossessed little boys—they'd wanted hard, strong bodies and hands that knew exactly how best to please them. He shook his head, aware of the dangers in baring a soul which necessity had clothed in secrecy many years before.

'Everyone knows what British boarding-schools are like,' he said dismissively.

'Not unless they've been to one, they don't. And I haven't. So I don't. Tell me, Luke!'

He shrugged. 'It's a system which works well on many levels,' he conceded levelly. 'So it isn't necessarily *bad*—just *different*.'

Holly smiled. 'It's okay—you don't have to defend the status quo to me, you know.'

She was chipping away with her persistence, each soft word exposing the hard, cold core of pain he had hidden away for so long.

'So which particular aspect would you like me to reveal to you?' he demanded. 'The isolation? The lack of physical warmth? The total lack of time to just sit and think? The disgusting food? The freezing dormitories?

The even more freezing early-morning showers which followed the equally freezing cross-country runs?'

'You must have been pretty fit,' she observed slowly, and cast him a long look from beneath lashes which could not quite obscure the glittering of her eyes.

Luke started. Of all the things she *could* have said... He had expected and been dreading the kind of cloying sympathy which most women seemed so comfortable with. Not a light, teasing kind of comment delivered with a little glint in her eye which made the slow pulsing of his desire escalate into an insistent pounding.

This was a game he was familiar with...

He bent his legs, just in case his exquisite hardness would be revealed to damn him. He needed to get out of here fast, but first he needed to kill that desire stone dead. And the only way he could think of doing that was by getting Holly and her long, long legs out of his line of vision.

'How about some coffee?' he suggested throatily, as his vocal cords joined in with his body's conspiracy by telling her how much he wanted her.

Coffee? Holly was both startled and disappointed. She wanted much more than coffee. She wanted *him*. And she wanted him badly—just as she had done from the moment she had first set eyes on him. When she had experienced an attraction towards him which had started with a thunderbolt and just continued to grow.

She had thought that he felt something for her, too— if not exactly the same in terms of intensity, then something very similar. Or had she simply been imagining that raw gleam of hunger which sometimes illuminated his eyes with a deep blue radiance? The easy companionship they had shared during her time at his house? Easy enough for her to think that there might be something more than just friendship…

Shakily, and trying to use as much grace as possible—which wasn't easy, given the length of her skirt—Holly rose to her feet and stood looking down at him.

'Coffee it is, then,' she said quietly, but still she didn't move, and there was a question in her eyes.

During his life, Luke had faced the very real adversities of hunger and pain and physical danger—and yet now he found himself in a situation far more threatening. He had a will of steel, forged by need in the long, lonely hours of his childhood, and yet that will now seemed to have deserted him.

He put his hand out towards her, and looked at it with bemused detachment, as if that hand were not under his control any more. It alighted on the slender curve of her ankle, and he felt the tiny shudder which thrilled her flesh as he made that first contact.

Slowly, lingeringly, he let his hand move upwards, so that it encircled her calf, and that calf suddenly seemed like the most erotic zone he had ever encountered. He let his middle finger trickle along the silken swell, in a way that made his body shudder as he imagined the natural path for that finger to now travel…

Holly didn't dare move, didn't dare speak, some instinct telling her that to do either would be to break this bewitching spell he had cast on her. His hand felt like the centre of a furnace. Or maybe his touch had transformed *her* into a furnace—for she could feel a fire beginning to blaze at the fork of her legs, the honeyed wetness which followed doing nothing to quench the remorseless heat building up inside her.

Luke's hand reached her knee. Never had he felt such an erotic contrast between bone and velvet-soft skin. He felt for the fleshy pocket behind the knee itself and sighed with pleasure. Using his thumb, he circled the skin there, round and round, over and over, until he felt it tremble helplessly beneath his touch. His hand crept inexorably upwards; he knew where he wanted to touch her most and, from the give-away little sag of her knees, he knew that she wanted it, too.

He knelt before her then, tightening his arms around her bottom, burying his face in the softness of her belly through the filmy voile of her dress. He felt her sway, and pulled her down so that she was kneeling, too, their eyes almost on a level, her expression one of breathless curiosity as she waited to see what he would do next.

Her eyes had never looked greener—luminous and bright as leaves which had just been rained on—nor more inviting. He saw her lips pucker helplessly, noted that the lush, dark lashes were in danger of fluttering to a close.

'I want to kiss you,' he told her, in a voice which sounded as heavy and as sweet as syrup.

'Then kiss me,' she managed drowsily, half despairing of her passivity.

'God, yes…' He would have kissed her anyway, invitation or not, for it would have been impossible to resist those lips. He lowered his mouth slowly… brushing it against hers with the merest whisper of contact…and Holly felt her lips part immediately.

Steadying himself with a hand now buried in the rip-

pling copper ropes of her hair, Luke deepened the kiss
with his tongue and felt her meet it, matching his own
passion and need, and yet inciting it further…demanding
more…

Fireworks threatened to explode inside his head and
in his aching groin, and he thought how intoxicating this
kiss was…

Intoxicating…

The word began to batter relentlessly at his conscience
like rain lashing against a window, and Luke felt his
body freeze with rejection, his lips stilling against hers.

For this was the act of a fool. This woman was like
a glass of champagne: the sudden high, the slaking of a
sensual thirst and then—what? The dry mouth, the headache and the regret of a hangover—that was what.

He was not in the market for any woman—but particularly not one who was everything he most feared and
despised in a woman. With her fey, enchanting beauty,
and all the restless inner energy of the creative person-
ality, she was the kind of woman who was bad news.
Very bad news indeed.

He plucked his mouth away from hers, and something
in his attitude must have unnerved her, for he saw the
sudden whitening of her face and the way that her eyes
had grown leaf-dark and startled.

And, even then, that treacherous protective instinct
which she alone seemed to inspire in him reared its interfering head once more, and he reached out automatically to steady her, afraid that she might simply crumple
to a heap in front of him.

'Luke—what on earth is the *matter*?' she demanded,
as she unseeingly let him gently propel her back towards

the sofa, where she slumped down like a puppet whose strings had just been cut. 'What are you *doing*?'

'I'm doing what I should have done about ten minutes ago,' he told her grimly. 'I'm leaving!'

'But why? I don't understand!'

'And you don't need to understand,' he gritted, his mouth hardening into an ugly line as he thought of how close he had come to...to... 'Forget it ever happened, Holly, because it meant *nothing*! It was an aberration, that's all.'

'An ''aberration''?' she challenged, then wished she hadn't because the look he threw her in response was insulting. 'What a *horrible* word!'

'Like me to explain it to you?' he queried, with silky condescension.

'I think I can just about work it out for myself, thank you!'

With the grace of a natural predator, he rose to his feet and came to stand over her, and Holly found that the trembling simply would not leave her. From her position on the sofa, Holly thought that his towering height made him look impossibly intimidating.

And distant.

Their eyes met, and in hers remained a query he could not ignore.

'That wasn't in my general scheme of things,' he told her brutally, in answer to the unasked question.

'You mean that *kiss*?' she demanded, her voice incredulous. Why was he making her feel like some night-club stripper over a simple *kiss*? 'Is that all?'

'*All?* Kisses like that generally lead on to something else, but I'm sure you don't need me to tell you that.'

His eyes were wintry. 'But maybe that's why you invited me up here? To ''christen'' the new flat in the way you like best?'

'You flatter yourself,' she observed furiously.

He shook his head. 'I don't think so.' A muscle began to work in his cheek as she frantically pulled at the hemline of her dress. 'Or are you denying that we've had the hots for each other since the moment we first met?'

So she *hadn't* been imagining it! 'No, I'm not denying it!' she told him, as she sat up straight and looked at him, her voice softening as she said, 'It isn't a crime!'

'No, it's just sex,' he told her. 'And that's *all* it is, Holly!'

'Sex?' she demanded. '*Sex?* What an insulting thing to say!'

He made an impatient movement with his hands. 'Call it chemistry, then—or mutual attraction. Whatever words you want to use if the truth offends you.' His voice dropped to a throaty whisper. 'And it's powerful, this feeling—I don't deny that. Potent as hell itself—but nebulous. Insubstantial. It peaks and then it wanes and leaves all kinds of havoc and destruction in its wake.'

Anger laced her voice with sarcasm. 'Aren't you overstating your case a little?'

He shook his tawny head. 'Am I? I don't think so, Holly. All I know is that I've had a fortnight of torture, of watching you move with that unconscious grace you have. Of imagining you undressing in the room down the hall from me. I've had to contend with the sight of you drifting around in one of *my* robes, knowing that you're buck-naked underneath, and I've had to stay sane and control my baser impulses. And it's been hard.'

Or, rather, *I've* been hard, he thought ruefully. Bad choice of word, Luke. 'But now that you're safely settled in your new home, our paths need hardly cross. And I think that's for the best.'

Best for *whom?* she almost yelled, but suspected she already knew the answer to that one. There was just one question she needed to ask him. 'Why, Luke?' And then she plucked up courage to add, 'When we both want to.'

But he shook his head, steeling himself against that plaintive little appeal. 'Why spend time going over it—when the outcome will remain the same? My reasons are both simple and complex and you don't need to know them.'

'Well, that's bloody *insulting* to me!' she stormed.

He raised his eyebrows. It was the only time he had ever heard her swear, and the zeal with which she did it only reinforced all his prejudices. The shutters came crashing down and he clicked out of emotion and into formality. Old habits died hard...

'Thank you for inviting me to your opening,' he finished politely. 'And I wish you every good fortune in your new endeavour. Goodnight, Holly.'

Still sitting collapsed on the sofa, her long legs sprawled in front of her, made Holly feel at a definite disadvantage, but she was damned if she was going to stumble to her feet to show him out. She would be bound to fall flat on her face, or something equally humiliating.

She gave him an unfriendly smile, his kindness to her forgotten in the face of sexual frustration and the accompanying rejection and bewilderment. 'Thanks for everything, Luke,' she told him insincerely. 'But you'll forgive me if I don't show you out.'

CHAPTER EIGHT

IT WAS just very fortunate that starting a new business meant that there were always a hundred and one things to think about, and to do—and for that Holly was extremely grateful. At least it meant that she didn't allow her mind to get stuck on that frustrating loop which wanted to know just why Luke Goodwin had:

a) Kissed her (and more)
b) Then acted as though she had some kind of infectious disease; and
c) Had disappeared conclusively from her life in the days following the opening of her shop.

She supposed that she could have picked up the telephone, or even gone round to his house, to ask the great man in person—but she had her pride. Luke wasn't a man she could imagine being railroaded into anything, and she certainly wasn't going to march round to beg him to make love to her!

So she forced herself to be sensible, filed all these unanswered questions away under 'Waste of Time', and resolutely refused to dwell on them further. Even though she missed him. Missed him like mad.

She had a few long, sleepless nights asking herself what had gone wrong, and why. Then she came to the conclusion that, since she wasn't going to get any answers, then there wasn't much point asking the questions. It was a useful safety mechanism.

Then she happened to bump into Luke's cleaning lady, Margaret, in the general store.

Margaret smiled encouragingly at her, and Holly plucked up courage to ask, very casually, 'How's Luke?'

'I wouldn't know, dear,' Margaret replied, with the repressed excitement of someone who knew that the person who had asked the question was hanging onto every word. 'He's gone away!'

Holly nearly dropped her organic wholemeal loaf on the floor. *'Gone?'* she echoed in horror. 'Gone *where*?'

'He didn't say, dear. Just upped and left the day after your shop opened, I think it was.'

'And is he coming back?' asked Holly, her heart feeling like a leaden weight in her chest.

Margaret shrugged. 'I expect so. He hasn't taken much—apart from his passport.'

'His *passport*?' repeated Holly, like a parrot.

'That's right.'

'But you don't know where he's gone?'

''Fraid I don't dear.' A mischievous gleam entered Margaret's rheumy eyes. 'Shall I say you was asking?'

'Er, no,' said Holly quickly. She flashed her most beseeching smile. 'I'd rather you didn't, Margaret.'

The article about Lovelace Brides had appeared in the *Winchester Echo* and captured the public's imagination. The people of Hampshire loved the story of Holly winning a wedding dress competition and opening a bridal shop—and then offering the same wedding dress as the prize in *another* competition!

It had proved so popular that it had been picked up

by the national press, including one of the broadsheets as well as three tabloids. In a week where news was scant, journalists and photographers were dispatched to Woodhampton, where Holly posed standing next to the dress, trying like mad to pin a happy-go-lucky smile to her lips.

It was fabulous publicity for her, and she knew that she *should* feel overjoyed—it was just very annoying to feel so deflated. Especially over a man she had foolishly imagined had shared her feelings.

Which only went to prove that her imagination was best left to dreaming up wedding dresses, and not romantic scenarios with would-be suitors.

Lured by the competition, brides-to-be flocked into the shop in what became an unusually busy December. It was traditionally a slack month—too many parties and too much preparation for Christmas leaving brides with little enthusiasm for buying their wedding dresses. With the added inches from too much merry-making, they tended to leave that until the New Year.

As the steady stream of customers filed into the shop, Holly soon realised that she was going to have to recruit more outworkers than she had originally anticipated. She needed workers who were good enough to sew her intricate designs and close enough for her to be able to keep an eye on them. She scribbled out an advertisement and put it in the *Echo*.

On a dull Monday morning, a couple of weeks before Christmas, Holly was rearranging her window display when she saw a woman standing waiting on the pavement outside, trying to catch her attention.

'Are you open?' mouthed the woman, pointing exaggeratedly at her watch.

'Not until ten!' Holly mouthed back, then wondered why she was sounding so inflexible. It was her business, and she could open when she liked! With a final twist of fern, which Michelle had concocted into a huge, old-fashioned bouquet with white silk roses, Holly jumped down out of the window and went to unlock the door.

'Come in,' she smiled.

'You're not supposed to be open until ten, are you?' murmured the woman, but she stepped into the shop anyway and looked around. She was wearing dark corduroy trousers, a green padded jacket and wellington boots. She wore the traditional country clothes well—they suited her clear skin and her neat, butter-coloured hair. She was trim, with tiny wrists and tiny ankles—the sign, or so Holly had been told by her mother, of a true lady.

'You're only ten minutes off, and the shop is still very new,' said Holly with a smile. 'I need to build up a reputation, and it wouldn't do mine much good if I forced you to stand outside in the cold, instead of bringing you in here and letting you browse around. I'm presuming that you *are* a bride-to-be?'

'I most certainly am!' giggled the woman. It was an attractive, infectious laugh, but a little girlish, too. And maybe just a tad inappropriate for someone pushing thirty, Holly thought. Until she reminded herself sternly that she was here to make wedding dresses, not value judgements! Still, she would bet, with a giggle like that, that this woman would go for flounces and frills and a bouquet as big as the Blackwall Tunnel!

'When,' asked Holly immediately, 'is the wedding?'

The woman pursed her lips together in a smile. 'Well, we haven't quite decided yet—you know what men are for making a commitment! My fiancé came over without me—to get everything ready,' she added with a coy shrug.

'But you're not planning a sudden Valentine wedding, are you?' asked Holly quickly. 'Because if you are, we'll have to get a move on.'

The woman shook her head. 'Oh, no! My fiancé and I haven't actually discussed a date—but I want to be sure that, when we do, I'll be ready to go!'

Keen, thought Holly with a smile. But, there again, so many brides were—and it would be a little disappointing if they weren't! 'Then we'd better introduce ourselves,' she said. 'I'm Holly Lovelace—owner and designer.'

'Caroline,' said the blonde, holding her hand out. 'Caroline Casey. I'm afraid that I'm a novice at all this—what do I do now?'

'You take a look at all those sample gowns hanging over there on the rail, and decide which ones you like the look of. Then you try them on, see which suits and whether you want any modifications made, and then I can have it made to measure.'

'And do they all have price tags?'

Holly nodded. 'Yes, they do.' Not all shops carried prices on their gowns, but it had been a conscious decision of hers to do so, because nothing was worse than falling madly in love with a wedding dress, only to discover that it was much more than you could afford. Holly knew that brides rarely looked too closely at a gown which was financially out of their reach. 'But if you're on a budget and particularly like a certain design, then we can sometimes have it made up in a less expensive fabric.'

'Oh, no!' Caroline laughed delicately, showing teeth which were straight and white and even—teeth which told of a lifetime's good nutrition, of sunshine and milk and no sweets to cause cavities. 'Money's certainly no object.' She paused and gave Holly a helpless little shrug. 'My fiancé has just come into a very large inheritance!'

Blinking away a brief but distracting feeling of *déjà vu*, Holly managed to smile, even though she thought the woman sounded more than a little smug. 'Good for him! And for you!' she added robustly, supposing that it was difficult to talk about a large inheritance *without* sounding smug. 'Nice to be in love,' she said wistfully. 'And it's probably even nicer if he's rich into the bargain!'

'Oh, I'd never have agreed to marry him if he hadn't come into money,' said Caroline, smiling and shaking her head when she saw the look of horror on Holly's face. 'Oh, no! I don't mean that I'm marrying him *just* for the money—although I have to agree, it helps! It's just that money brings with it responsibilities. And, more importantly, stability. And my fiancé was pretty wild before he inherited!' She wrinkled up her pretty nose. '*Very* wild!'

The mind boggled. 'In what way?' asked Holly curiously.

'In every way.' Caroline shrugged. 'The original rolling stone!'

Holly smiled, feeling a sneaking sympathy for the man. She suspected that the pretty but determined Caroline Casey would keep her errant fiancé on a very short rein indeed! 'Listen—why don't I make us some coffee and leave you to browse through the dresses at your leisure?'

'That's very sweet of you.'

When Holly came back with coffee, it was *her* turn to feel smug, since the woman had done exactly as she'd predicted and picked out the most frothy, fairy-princess dress on the rail! It had a low, flounced neck, a jewel-encrusted bodice, nipped waist and a skirt wide enough to hide a family of six beneath its voluminous silk folds.

Holly didn't just design dresses that she was passionate about—she also designed dresses to sell. You had to if you were a businesswoman, or so her favourite tutor had told her at college. And frothy, traditional dresses *did* sell—no doubt about it, there was always a market for them.

Caroline experimentally held the dress up in front of her. 'Do you like it?'

'Your waist is going to look like Scarlett O'Hara's in that,' promised Holly truthfully.

Caroline clutched the dress to her. 'I've dreamed of a wedding dress like this one ever since I was a little girl!'

'Well, that's what tends to happen.' Holly smiled. 'Just so long as you aren't marrying a man who wants you to elope in a short red dress on the back of his motorbike!'

Caroline frowned. 'I think that's what most men *would* like, if the truth were known. Men don't like a lot of fuss, do they?'

Holly had learnt to agree with the customer—up to a point. 'Generally speaking, no.'

'But I'm a great believer in tradition,' said Caroline firmly.

'But not tradition simply for the sake of it, surely?' the imp in Holly argued back.

Caroline fixed her with a look of mild amusement. 'Most certainly I do. Tradition is the bedrock of society—the fabric that binds us together and links us with our past. Now...' she ran her finger along a ruffle of lace on one of the sleeves '...can I go and try this on?'

'Please do,' said Holly. 'The changing room is over here. What shoe size are you?'

'Only four.' Caroline gave a little wriggle of her shoulders as she projected a dainty foot forward like a ballet dancer. 'I'm only little, I'm afraid.'

'Then take these shoes with you—and call me if you need me,' said Holly gently, and drew back the velvet curtain to the changing room. She found herself wondering why Caroline had no one with her. Brides rarely came looking for gowns alone—they generally brought their mother or a best friend. Someone close enough to be brutally honest when asked the universal question, Does my bottom look big in this?

While Caroline was in the changing room, Holly hunted around for more accessories—veil and headdress—which she thought might go well with the dress.

And when Caroline reappeared, looking a little self-conscious in all her finery, Holly experienced the familiar feeling of awe and wonder at how a wedding dress could transform a woman into a goddess. Women *stood* differently in a wedding dress. *Walked* differently.

'That ivory silk does wonders for your complexion,' she told her admiringly.

Caroline twirled in front of the floor-to-ceiling mirror. 'Does it? It's beautiful,' she said breathlessly. 'I feel just like a fairy princess!'

'It's much too big around the waist. Here—let me take it in a bit.' Pins on her wristband, Holly crouched down and adjusted the waist and then the hem.

While she was making her alterations, Holly chatted and listened. Women opened up to their dressmakers, and Caroline was no exception. By the end of the fitting, Holly was left with the impression that Caroline was a pleasant and competent woman, but grindingly dull and conventional!

It was getting on for lunch-time when the bride-to-be came out of the changing room, an ordinary woman once more in her cords and sweater. Holly looked up from the ivory silk and smiled at her. 'So what made you choose my little shop in Woodhampton for your wedding dress?'

'Nothing more inspiring than geography, I'm afraid.' Caroline found a compact inside her handbag, and, peering into the mirror, began to pat the shine off her neat little nose. 'I'm going to be living here, you see.'

'Oh? Whereabouts?'

'In Woodhampton itself.' Caroline's voice became injected with pride. 'There's a rather nice Georgian house in the village,' she confided. 'Apson House. I expect you know it.'

For a moment Holly's heart missed a beat while the world stopped turning. Either that or she would wake up in a moment. She felt all the blood draining from her face, and wondered whether she had a corresponding colour loss. 'Yes, I know it,' she replied, in a muffled voice which seemed to come from a different pair of lungs than hers. Then forced herself to ask the question, as if she didn't already know the answer, 'And wh-who's your fiancé?'

Caroline frowned, antennae alerted by the fine beads of sweat sheening Holly's brow. 'It's Luke,' she said precisely, her pale grey gaze piercing. 'Luke Goodwin. Do you know him?'

Holly was experiencing sensations she had only ever read about. Head like cotton wool. Legs like jelly. Stomach turned to water. She was terribly afraid that she might faint. And meanwhile the unbelievable fact was hammering into her brain. *Luke Goodwin was engaged to be married to the grindingly dull Caroline Casey!*

Luke Goodwin was a no-good *deceiving bastard*!

'*Do you know him?*' repeated Caroline ominously, sounding as if she were counsel for the prosecution, and Holly were on the witness stand.

Well, she couldn't lie. Margaret, Luke's cleaner, knew that she had been staying up at the house while the shop was being renovated, and so did everyone else in the village. 'Yes, I know him,' she answered steadily.

Caroline looked at her wordlessly, her eyebrows raised in expectation.

'You see, I was…I was staying up at Apson House—'

'You were *what*?' came the disbelieving snap.

'Just for a couple of weeks—'

'A couple of *weeks*?' Caroline's eyes were spitting fire. 'Perhaps you'd care to explain?'

Holly swallowed. 'This shop and the flat above it were

in the most dreadful state when I arrived, and Luke kind of came to the rescue. He had to sack the agent and there was nowhere habitable for me to stay—that's why he put me up.'

'And why would he do that?' Caroline asked, in a voice of quiet menace.

'Because he owns the freehold of this building—but you probably knew that already.'

Caroline's mouth had thinned into a sarcastic line. 'I'm afraid that my knowledge of Luke's life in England is somewhat patchy—certainly when compared to yours. You must fill me in, Holly. Just how *well* do you actually know Luke?'

Holly stared at her. The inference was clear. 'What do you mean, exactly?'

'I'll tell you *exactly* what I mean!' Caroline put her head forward, like a tortoise emerging from its shell and blinked rapidly at Holly. 'Luke is a man with certain, shall we say…appetites? And he's a little old-fashioned at heart. You know, one of those men who marry a woman because they love and respect her, but who will avail themselves of an attractive substitute should the need arise—if you'll forgive the pun,' she finished maliciously. 'So did he?'

Holly's throat was so tight she could scarcely breathe, let alone speak, but somehow she forced the words out. 'Did he what?'

'Did he sleep with you?'

Only in her tortured and exquisite dreams. 'How dare you ask me that?'

There was a pause. Caroline looked her straight in the eye. 'I'll ask you again, Holly. I'm a very understanding woman, you know, and sex has nothing to do with re-spect—especially where Luke is concerned. Did you sleep with him?'

Thoughts buzzed into Holly's mind like sandflies, but the most disturbing dominated all the others. She could hear Caroline saying it defiantly, almost proudly: 'Oh, I'd never have agreed to marry him if he hadn't come into money.'

She met Caroline's gaze without blushing. Guided solely by instinct coloured with a gut feeling of pure *indignation*, Holly realised that with her next words she could wreck her reputation. But she had gambled every-thing else—why not her reputation? 'I stayed in his house for days,' she replied, with slow deliberation. 'And you know Luke. What do you think?'

'I'll tell you what I think! I think you're deluding yourself if you think you stand any chance with him.' Caroline gave her a smile which was almost sympa-thetic. 'Because Luke was always rather bored by any woman who was such an easy lay!'

CHAPTER NINE

AFTER Caroline had flounced out of the shop, telling Holly exactly what she could do with her wedding dress, Holly went through to the kitchen at the back and sat down, her hands trembling, her nerves shot to pieces by what Luke's fiancée—Luke's *fiancée*!—had just told her, and by the enormity of what she had done in retaliation.

Luke was engaged to be married.

That was the one fact which overrode every other thought. Crucial.

But even more crucial was the fact that he had deceived her. He had lied by omission. He had allowed an easy companionship to develop, and had ignited the flames of sexual desire when he could have effectively doused them completely by telling her the simple truth.

That he was engaged to be married.

Holly buried her head in her hands as she thought about him and found that she wanted to weep—she who never wept. Who as a child had constantly kept the non-committal smile expected of her, even when her life had been torn up by the roots, time and time again.

It was bad enough that he had lied. Bad enough that he had chosen to commit himself to someone who, yes, Holly could see, had all the attributes of a good wife. Caroline was intelligent enough. Neat, organised, attractive, and determined but, *oh*...how could a man like

128

Luke—*Luke*—be contemplating spending the rest of his life with her?

Because even worse than the pain of his deceit was the pain of knowing why he had pushed her away, and why he had stayed out of her life in the days since that frustrating encounter. For he wasn't hers, and he never would be. Holly had finally met a man she would change her life for, but he belonged to somebody else.

But businesswomen couldn't hurl themselves to the ground and drum their feet in anger and frustration, which was what she *felt* like doing! There wasn't even a packet of biscuits to defiantly plough her way through—not that she really wanted to start comfort eating at *this* stage in her life.

Instead, she spent the afternoon sewing her first full order—a gown for a Christmas wedding, with a full white taffeta skirt and a buttoned bodice in deep forest-green velvet. The tiny bridesmaids' dresses had the pattern reversed, with velvet skirts and taffeta bodices, and Michelle was going to make mistletoe and holly coronets.

She was undisturbed for the most part, with just two customers wandering in. Young women who said that they wanted to browse. They also wanted to enter the free draw for the prize-winning dress, which Holly suspected was their main reason for coming into the shop!

They filled out their cards respectively, and dropped them into the slightly garish red satin box which Holly had provided.

'When's it being drawn?' asked one.

'New Year's Day,' answered Holly with a faint smile.

'At the stroke of midnight?' asked the other hopefully.

'Like Cinderella, you mean?' Holly smiled properly then. Your emotional world could collapse around you, and yet romance never seemed to die. Thank heavens. 'Why not?' She shrugged.

The rest of the afternoon dragged like Christmas Eve to a child. At four o'clock she was longing to shut up shop and go upstairs. There were accounts which needed to be sorted out and she could put the finishing touches to the green velvet wedding dress in comfort. Enough to keep her busy for the rest of the evening, anyway. That was if she could resist the temptation to crawl beneath the duvet and just wish that the world would go away.

She was just tucking a frilly blue garter to the back of a drawer when the shop bell rang and she looked up, her words dying on her lips when she saw who it was.

Her first thought was that it didn't really look like Luke at all, since he was wearing an unfamiliar deep blue suit and a silk tie of palest blue. A *tie*! *Luke*! She would never have imagined him wearing such fine wool and silk, though it came as no surprise to see how well the formal clothes fitted his rugged frame. But the impeccably cut outfit had the effect of distancing him, making him look like some cool and devastating stranger.

Luke quietly closed the door behind him and then locked it, and something about his face and the rigid set of his shoulders made Holly run her tongue over her lips and say nervously, 'What do you think you're doing?'

'What does it look like? I'm locking the door.'

'But we're still open!' she objected, her pulse picking up speed like a racehorse. 'You can't do that.'

'Oh, can't I?' He turned round then, and the shadowed

fury which darkened his features made Holly freeze with apprehension.

'Just watch me, sweetheart,' he drawled, and he began to walk towards her.

Holly correctly read the menace and determination in that walk, and some mad, unthinking part of her wanted to run away from him. She found herself looking frantically from side to side, as though a trapdoor would suddenly appear and she would be able to make her escape.

Luke could see her anxiety, but he felt not a jot of pity for her, only the anger which had burned through his veins all afternoon and which was threatening to consume him.

He was directly in front of her now, and Holly saw that he was controlling his breathing only with great difficulty.

'What are you doing here?' she whispered, her voice sounding like a husky croak.

It was the wrong thing to say. His mouth curved into a thin parody of a smile which chilled her.

'You know damn well what I'm doing here.'

'I d-don't.'

He drew a breath as though he were taking in poison. 'What exactly did you tell Caroline?'

'You mean your fiancée?' she bit back.

'Answer me, you little bitch!'

The insult first rocked her, then filled her with the fury to fight him back.

'I told her the truth!'

'You're lying, Holly.' He was itching to grab her by the shoulders, to haul her up against his chest and extract every raw, painful word of what she had actually told Caroline. And then?

'You weren't there,' she pointed out.

'I didn't need to be.'

'Well, then.' She shrugged. 'It's her word against mine—whatever she's told you.'

Her audacity momentarily stunned him. 'I'll tell you what she *told* me, sweetheart. That you and I apparently slept together.' He gave a cold, empty laugh. 'Strange, that—the earth can't have moved for either of us, since I don't actually remember doing it.'

Doing it. Holly felt the hot rush of excitement and prayed for it to pass. She shook her head in an effort to distract herself. 'I didn't *tell* her that I slept with you,' she contradicted. 'That was her accusation.' Her lashes lowered by a fraction to partially conceal her eyes, but she was certain that he had read the longing there. 'An accusation which she found impossible not to believe was true.'

'Particularly as you refused to deny it?' he suggested, with icy calm.

Holly shrugged. 'There was no point in denying it. Since *Caroline*—' she spat the word out, appalled at herself for doing so and yet unable to prevent the anger which was still distorting her voice '—had already made her mind up. And she seemed to find it unbelievable that you and I had managed to remain under one roof for a fortnight without having sex!'

He found it pretty unbelievable himself, come to think of it, but that was beside the point. 'What right do you think you have to start meddling in my life?' he demanded. 'How *dare* you let Caroline believe that we had been intimate?'

Holly had had enough. He was acting as if there had been nothing between them—as if the camaraderie which had grown up between them had not existed! 'But we *were* intimate! You know we were!'

His mouth twisted. 'I'm sorry? Have we been existing in parallel universes, or is there something I have missed? Just *when* are we supposed to have been intimate?'

She felt as if she was floundering in a dark, cold pool of misunderstanding. She remembered the touch of his hand on her ankle, the way she had drawn in a breath and looked down at him. Their gazes had locked the instant before they'd kissed, and something momentous had happened—surely he wasn't going to deny *that*?

'You *touched* me!' she protested throatily. 'You know you did!'

'I touched you?' he echoed in disbelief. 'And you think that gives you carte blanche to try to take control of my life by implying that there had been so much more than that? What right do you have to do that, Holly?'

She shook her head distractedly, copper curls spilling like corkscrews over her shoulders. 'But there are other kinds of intimacies, too—the little, unspoken ones. We grew close when I stayed with you, Luke—you know we did! You even admitted it! If you'd been honest with me *then*, and told me about Caroline, there would have been a completely different atmosphere between us! An atmosphere which would not have given rise to that kiss.' She drew a deep shuddering breath. 'So why *didn't* you tell me, Luke? Just answer me that?'

He gave an arrogant smile. 'You didn't ask.' But that wasn't the full story, and he knew it. He hadn't wanted to tell her, hadn't wanted to say the words out loud because that would have meant acknowledging reality, and it had been sweet indeed to pretend that reality didn't exist. It had been wonderful having Holly around. He had been enjoying the warmth of her company, and that was a fact. Enjoying the easy atmosphere coupled with the excitement of knowing that he couldn't have her...

'I can't believe you didn't even *mention* a girlfriend!'

His eyes glittered in legitimate challenge. 'Well, maybe you should have asked me.'

'That's not fair and you know it!' she objected hotly.

'Isn't it?' His eyes were azure spotlights which fixed her in their glare. 'Then let's just say that I didn't want to stray into the dangerous waters of the deeply personal.'

'But you told me all about your mother—and you can't get more personal than that!'

'That's different!' he snarled, remembering her gentle questions, the careless way she had shrugged at his reluctance to answer, so that—perversely—he had wanted to tell her. And then the way that it had all seemed to come pouring out of him, like the bursting of a dam. Disturbing. And especially disturbing for a man like Luke who had grown up with no one to confide in, who had convinced himself that it was better like that. That feelings should be locked out of sight and out of harm's way. When you were the only motherless boy in an English boarding-school, it was easier like that...

Holly gave a bitter laugh as she saw the shuttered look which had given him the face of a dark, beautiful statue.

'I used to wonder why you hadn't jumped on me like most men try to—'

'Did that disappoint you, then?' he enquired silkily. 'Do you like being jumped on, Holly?'

She ignored the crude taunt. 'I *thought* it was because you were a gentleman and that you respected me, but now I see I couldn't have been more wrong! You're a bastard, Luke Goodwin—to make a promise to one woman, and then to flirt like crazy with another!'

A pulse began to flicker ominously in his cheek. 'If I had flirted like crazy, then you would have known all about it, sweetheart,' he ground out. 'And the bottom line is that we kissed. Nothing more. Like you said yourself at the time, as I recall.' His mouth twisted with agonised desire. 'Though, quite frankly, if you wear skirts as short as the one you had on that day then—'

'Then I can expect men to lose all control?' she put in. 'Is that what you were about to say, Luke? That I was asking for it?'

'But I *didn't* lose control, did I?' he retorted. 'I stopped at a kiss, though God knows how, since you weren't just asking for it, Holly, you were simply *begging* for it—'

That did it! 'You *bastard*!' There was a loud crack as her palm connected with his cheek, and they both looked at one another, aware that an unbreachable line had just been crossed.

Luke felt desire and anger bubbling up in a heady cocktail inside him as he slowly rubbed his reddening cheek. 'So that's the way you want it, is it, sweetheart?'

Holly looked at him, powerless to resist the primitive emotions which were swirling so powerfully in the air around them. 'Luke…' she began, but he shook his head, and something in his eyes silenced her words, though he could do nothing to still the shuddering of her breath.

He moved to within a step away, his mouth a grim, forbidding line, the blue eyes dark as sapphires. 'Why did you let her think that I'd slept with you, Holly? Why did you let Caroline believe a lie like that?'

She pushed the feelings of guilt away. *He* was the one guilty of deceit. 'Haven't you stopped to ask just *why* she believed me? There doesn't seem much hope for a relationship if your fiancée is so willing to think that you'd be unfaithful at the first opportunity. Or maybe in the past you have been? Maybe she's judging you on past experience?'

'You think that of me?'

She heard the outrage and the surprise in his voice and shrugged. 'I don't know,' she told him tiredly. Her head was spinning so much she didn't seem to know anything any more.

'Well, I'd hate to disappoint you, sweetheart,' he drawled. 'So let me be the bastard of your dreams instead…'

She should have anticipated what was coming next from the heat which burned in the depths of his eyes, and the husky note which had deepened his voice to rich, dark velvet. But she had thought that he might be restrained by the fact that they were standing in the middle of the shop, for all the world to see, reflected three times over by the vast mirrors which lined the walls, with the chandelier spilling golden nuggets of light onto their heads.

'Luke—' she whispered again, but he pulled her into his arms and roughly, brutally, almost punishingly began to kiss her. 'Luke, no!'

This was wrong. She knew it was wrong for lots and lots of reasons—so why was she allowing herself to be swept along by the power of his kiss? 'Stop it,' she beseeched in a whisper against the softness of his lips, but it was a meaningless entreaty and they both knew it. 'Stop it, Luke.'

'Make me,' he whispered back, following his words with a provocative little lick at the roof of her mouth, and Holly swayed in his arms, laced her fingers into the thick, gold-tipped richness of his hair as she had wanted to for so long that it seemed a lifetime of wanting. 'Go on—*make* me...'

Very deliberately, he moved his hands from her narrow back and splayed them proprietorially over her buttocks, bringing her right against him. Then he slowly began to circle his hips in the most blatantly provocative way, letting her feel the hard, butting ridge of his desire.

She felt him, and jerked with a spasm of shock and excitement. 'Luke...' said Holly weakly, as his lips continued their relentless onslaught, overloading her senses until she could barely think at all, let alone think straight.

'What?' Moving one hand from her bottom, he allowed his fingers to trickle with agonising slowness up towards her breasts, and he heard her long sigh of surrender even as he felt her body melt against him. He opened his eyes and saw their reflection in one of the huge mirrors, their bodies glued together—and it turned him on unbearably.

She was wearing a long, flowing velvet skirt in richest

burgundy and a floaty white chiffon shirt. With it she
wore a matching burgundy bodice which fitted as closely
as a glove, with lots of tiny, velvet-covered buttons all
the way down the front. Her hair flowed like a river of
copper curls down her back, caught back from her face
by two tortoiseshell combs. With her white skin and emerald eyes, he thought that she looked as if she had
stepped out of a painting from another century.

'Luke, please...' she pleaded, without knowing what
it was she was asking him for.

He gave a low laugh tinged with passion and power.
He had her right where he wanted her. 'What?' he whispered again, and Holly was too befuddled to hear the
mocking tone which coloured his voice.

Luke turned his attention to the bodice, snapping open
first one button and then another, making a small groan
of frustration beneath his breath as he saw just how
many buttons there were. This was going to take for ever
and he didn't want to wait. He wanted to tear the clothes
from her body, to reveal those lush, creamy breasts and
then to take them in his mouth and suckle them. Bite
them and tease them until her head was thrown back and
through dry lips she would be demanding that he take
her, take away the remorseless aching.

'God, your breasts are beautiful,' he breathed, as another button flew open.

'O-oh.' She stumbled, as his thumb brushed over the
velvet, tantalising the nub which was thrusting against
the thick material.

'Don't you ever wear a bra?' he wanted to know, his
excitement rocketing as his fingers realised that there
was no scrap of silk or lace to restrain them....

'Never,' she managed weakly. Her fingers seemed to have a mind of their own as they moved possessively over his broad back, moving beneath his jacket and wantonly caressing the warm flesh through the silken shirt.

'Don't you know how much it turns men on?' he managed, finding that he wanted to outrageously demand that she always wore one in future. Unless she was with *him*... He pulled his mouth away from hers then, fighting for sanity through the mists of his desire. He would have to take her upstairs right now, because if he didn't...

A sudden banging at the door was like having a bucket of iced water hurled over her, and Holly found herself swaying in Luke's arms, blinking up at him in confusion.

'W-what's that?'

Luke had razor-sharp reflexes which had been honed over years of working in the reserve, and he had swiftly rebuttoned Holly's bodice and straightened it almost before she realised what was happening.

'You have a customer,' he mocked her darkly. 'Remember? This is a shop.'

And Holly looked towards the door in dismay, where a stocky young woman stood looking in. Her eyes flickered towards Luke's face for some kind of reassurance, but none was forthcoming. His features displayed all the disgust she might have expected from a man she had almost let make love to her in public. Oh, *Lord*, what had she *done*?

'Hadn't you better let her in?' asked Luke, his voice as distant as the wind.

And Holly went to unlock the door.

CHAPTER TEN

HOLLY'S first thought was that the young woman who stood outside didn't look a bit like a bride-to-be. Not just because she was plump—although plump brides tended to buy their dresses in the safe, anonymous atmosphere of the department store rather than specialist shops. Or because she wore no glittering engagement ring—lots of women chose not to wear *those*. Caroline had not worn one, she remembered, wincing.

No, it was the woman's general expression of harassment—she looked flustered and out of breath, and carried none of the satisfied glow of a woman about to choose her wedding dress.

'Are you sure you're open?' she asked, as Holly pulled the door open, her soft cheeks growing pink. And Holly found herself blushing too, as she wondered just how much of that passionate little bout with Luke the woman had witnessed. And speaking of Luke...

She glanced over her shoulder. Why was he still standing exactly where she had left him, like a dark, immovable force? Their eyes met—his still angry and glittering with frustration, while Holly felt totally compromised by that outrageously effective demonstration of his sexual skills. He had ruthlessly manipulated her, almost...almost... She glared at him but still he didn't budge.

'Yes, of course we're open,' smiled Holly brightly. 'Do come in.'

'Thanks.' The woman stepped into the shop and looked around, but again and again her attention kept coming back to the spotlit dress in the window.

Close up, Holly could see her plumpness couldn't detract from the most beautiful pair of dark blue eyes she had ever seen, with lashes so long you could have hung your washing from them. Her skin was all berries and cream, and she had a thick head of glossy black hair caught back in an old-fashioned chignon.

'I'm Holly Lovelace,' said Holly, holding out her hand.

The woman smiled and an irrepressible dimple appeared in her right cheek. 'Is that your real name?'

Holly nodded. 'It really is!'

'I'm Ursula O'Neil. Pleased to meet you.'

'And I'm Luke Goodwin,' came a silky dark voice from behind them.

Ursula turned round and beamed. 'Hello,' she said shyly.

'What sort of thing are you looking for?' asked Holly, glowering at Luke.

'Well, it's a bit difficult to explain...'

Holly asked her stock question for dithering brides. 'How do you see yourself on your wedding day?'

The woman shook her head. 'Oh, no! I'm not getting married. It's a bit of a funny old story...'

Glad to be distracted from Luke's brooding figure, and intrigued by the woman's hesitation, Holly gestured towards the velvet sofa. 'Look, why don't you sit down,' she suggested 'and tell me all about it?'

The woman looked across the shop at Luke. 'I don't want to disturb anything—'

'You aren't disturbing anything—*honestly*,' interjected Holly quickly—much *too* quickly, really. 'Luke was just going, weren't you, Luke?'

He gave her a bland smile as their eyes met. 'Actually no.' He smiled. 'I think I'll stay.'

Holly threw him a warning look. She wanted him *out. Now!* For how could she concentrate on anything when he was standing there like some dark, avenging angel, with that arrogant half-smile serving as a constant reminder of what they had been doing just a few moments ago?

'But the customer might prefer to speak to me in private,' she said icily.

Luke turned a hundred-watt smile on the woman and Holly knew immediately that she wouldn't stand a chance in hell of resisting him. 'You don't mind, do you, Ursula?'

Obediently the woman shook her head at him, melting under the impact of that mega-watt dazzle. 'No, I don't mind at all.' She settled herself on the velvet sofa, but her attention remained focussed on the window and she laced her fingers together nervously, before taking a deep breath. 'That dress you have in the window...'

Holly looked at her encouragingly as her words tailed off. 'Yes?'

'Is it...is it a very old dress?'

Holly looked at her in surprise. 'No, it isn't.'

'How old?'

'Well, I made it earlier this year.'

'*You* made it?'

Holly blinked. 'Yes, I did.'

'I see.' Ursula's face crumpled with disappointment and she began digging around in her handbag, eventually extracting a scrunched up tissue and loudly blowing her nose.

'Is something wrong?' asked Holly gently.

Ursula shook her head. 'No, nothing's wrong. It's just that I saw a picture of it in the newspaper, and I thought…I thought…'

'What did you think?' interposed Holly quietly.

'It looks exactly the same as a wedding dress my mother bought,' Ursula gulped, like a woman about to burst into tears. 'But of course it can't be!'

'No, it can't be.' Holly paused, then frowned as the facts began to piece themselves together in her mind like a jigsaw. 'This dress that your mother bought—when was that exactly? Can you remember?'

Ursula shrugged her fleshy shoulders. 'It'd be over twenty years ago now.' Her voice softened. 'It was in a sale at the big London store she worked in. She queued all night in the rain to buy it. It was for me, and for my sister—we were each to wear it when we got married…'

'And what happened to it?'

Ursula lifted her head proudly and looked Holly straight in the eye. 'My father died, and we had no money.' Her voice faltered. 'So she sold it. She put an advert in the paper. She had to. It broke my mother's heart to see it go.' She shrugged, her voice wobbling a little. 'But what use is a fine dress in the cupboard when there's no food on the table?'

'No use at all,' said Luke slowly, and they both turned round to look at him, as though they had forgotten he was there. But Luke, it seemed, had all the answers. 'Your mother bought the original dress, you see, Ursula.'

'Yes, of *course* she did!' breathed Holly slowly.

'I'm sorry?' Ursula looked at them both in confusion. 'I don't understand what it is you're saying.'

'That dress you see in the window, yes, *I* designed and made it,' explained Holly. 'But I based the design on one of my mother's original sketches—because she was a dress designer, too, and it was one of her favourite gowns. And *your* mother must have bought *my* mother's dress! Now do you see?'

'Heavens!' said Ursula.

Holly smiled. 'So, although the two dresses aren't exactly the same, they're very, very similar.'

Ursula stood up and moved closer to the window to look at the dress, her eyes as wide as saucers, like a child taken to the ballet for the very first time. 'Yes, they are,' she agreed. 'Very similar. Dear me, it's unbelievable!' She was silent for a moment as she stared at the soft satin. 'The dress used to hang in the wardrobe in our bedroom and we were allowed to look at it and touch it, but only through the plastic. Except on our birthdays, when she used to take it out of its covering and we were allowed a proper look at it. Oh, how we loved that dress!'

'And did your mother never even try it on?' asked Holly. 'Just to see what it looked like?'

Ursula shook her head. 'It was a tiny dress, and she was a big woman.' She glanced down at her generous curves with a rueful expression. 'Like me. She used to say that she wouldn't even be able to squeeze her fingers into the sleeves! But it would fit my sister, and she's getting married soon. It may not be the original, but it's the next best thing. That's why I came here today.' She pulled a purse from her bag as if she were about to start bartering down at the market and gave Holly a huge smile. 'To buy it.'

Holly didn't know what to say. Or rather she did, but she wasn't sure how best to phrase it without sounding cruel or hurtful.

'How much is it, please?' asked Ursula.

Holly shook her head. 'But I'm afraid it isn't for sale.'

Ursula frowned. 'I don't understand. It's in the window—'

'Yes, I know it is. But didn't you read the whole article? It's a bit of a stunt. I've only just opened the shop, and I'm offering the wedding dress as the prize in a draw. So, although you can't buy it, you're very welcome to enter into the draw to win it.'

Ursula bit her lip. 'But what if I don't win?'

'Well, if your sister desperately wants that particular design, then I can have one made up—but she won't be able to wear it until March.'

'March?' queried Ursula. 'But Amber is getting married in February! How come?'

Holly sighed. 'Because the bridal magazine who sponsored the competition are doing a whole big feature on the dress in the March edition—and part of the deal was that, if I sold it, then it could not be worn until after that edition has hit the shelves. They want the feature to have maximum impact, you see.'

'That would be a pretty difficult rule to enforce,' Luke reflected.

Holly frowned at him. 'Yes, I know it would! But it

would be pretty churlish not to abide by the competition rules, wouldn't it? Especially as their prize money financed my business in the first place!'

His eyes were thoughtful as they rested on Holly. 'You mean you'll abide by the spirit of the law as opposed to the letter?'

'That's exactly what I mean!'

Ursula gave a resigned shrug. 'Oh, well, then. I guess I'll put my name in the hat with the rest of them and say a prayer or two! It would be great to have the dress, even if Amber won't be able to wear it.'

'Do you have no idea who your mother sold the original to?' Luke asked.

Ursula shook her head. 'No idea at all. Mum kept it all pretty hush-hush. Selling off your possessions because you were short of money wasn't something you shouted from the rooftops—not where I came from, anyway.'

'And where's that?' queried Luke.

'South London. I live on the opposite side of town, these days.'

Luke nodded. 'And how are you getting back there tonight?'

Ursula shook her head. 'I'm not. I've booked in at The Bell. I don't like these country roads at night.'

'I don't blame you,' he said.

'Here.' Holly handed her one of the entry forms and Ursula filled in her name and address, then dropped it into the red satin box.

Afterwards she shook hands with both of them. 'It's been great meeting you both! And thank you for your help,' she said. 'Even if I don't win, it was interesting to learn a bit more of the dress's history.'

'I'll tell my mother when I next see her,' promised Holly. 'She usually turns up in England for Christmas!'

'I'd like to tell mine,' said Ursula with a sad smile. 'But she died a long time ago.'

'I'm so sorry,' said Holly. On an impulse, she picked up one of her cards from the counter and thrust it into Ursula's hand. 'If you ever need a wedding dress, then you know where I am.'

Ursula smiled. 'Thanks—but I'm hoping I might win that one!'

Holly hoped so, too—though she couldn't see what use it would be if she did. The prize-winning dress would never fit Ursula, and her sister would be getting married before it could legitimately be worn...

There was silence in the shop once she had gone, and it took every bit of Holly's courage to turn to Luke and say, 'Is that everything? Only I don't want to keep you.'

'Everything?' He laughed, but it was an angry, bitter kind of laugh, as though Ursula leaving the shop had negated any need for him to be pleasant to her. 'Sweetheart, I haven't even started yet. We may have just been treated to a touching story, but nothing has changed. Think back to what we were doing before Ursula arrived, Holly.'

Her cheeks flamed, even as her heart began to pick up speed. That was the *last* thing she wanted to do. 'Luke, I really think it's best if you go.'

'I'm sure you do. And we must always do what's best for Holly Lovelace, mustn't we?' A muscle began to work convulsively in his cheek. 'But damn the rest of the world, isn't that right?'

'I don't know what you're talking about.' She made to turn away but he wouldn't let her, grabbing her by the arm, and even that rough contact made her blood sing.

'Don't you?' He was staring deeply into her eyes, and Holly seemed paralysed, rooted to the ground, mesmerised by the magic of that dark denim-blue gaze.

'N-no.'

'Oh, I think you do, Holly. Be honest now.'

'I don't.' He was still holding tightly onto her arm, his expression a mixture of disdain and desire, and yet still she remained fixed to the spot. 'Let me go,' she protested ineffectually.

'No.' He tipped his gold-brushed head to one side and gave her a long, considering look. 'See what it feels like when someone takes control? You should do—after all, you're the ultimate control freak, aren't you, Holly? You decided that you wanted me, didn't you? You wanted me real *bad* and you weren't going to let anything as inconvenient as a fiancée in your way. That, presumably, is why you told her that we'd been sleeping together—'

'Luke, don't—'

'Don't what?' He raised his eyebrows mockingly. 'Don't tell the truth? But why ever not, Holly? Does the truth make you feel uncomfortable? And it is the truth, isn't it, Holly? *Isn't* it?'

'Y-yes,' she admitted brokenly. 'Partly.'

He nodded. 'Yes, I know what you mean—and it *is* only part of the truth, because of course we *haven't* slept together, have we, Holly? Not yet.'

His words sent shivers down her spine. 'That wasn't what I meant. Luke—'

'After all,' he interrupted remorselessly, 'you've got what you want now, haven't you? Caroline is off the scene. You made damn sure of that—'

'Caroline has *gone*?'

His mouth shaped itself into a cruel curve. 'Yes, she's *gone*!' he mimicked ruthlessly. 'Of course she's gone! Or did you imagine that she would hang around hoping that we could all have a cosy little threesome?'

'Don't be so disgusting!' she snapped.

'Oh, I can get a lot more disgusting than that, sweetheart!' he vowed, and Holly wondered how his pitiless words had managed to produce the tantalising excitement which was currently tiptoeing its way up her spine.

'But you probably like it that way, don't you?' he persisted. 'Isn't that what you got up to at art school? Threesomes? Perversions are all the rage, surely—and it would be so incredibly *bourgeois* not to join in, don't you think?'

'I don't have to stay here and listen to this!' she snapped, making to pull away from him, but he caught her other arm to pull her against his chest. His mouth descended on hers and all his anger and frustration and pent-up desire exploded in a fever of need which only matched hers.

One touch and she was lost.

She knew it and he knew it, and there didn't seem to be a damned thing she could do to stop it.

'Now kill the lights,' he growled.

And like a willing puppet she did as he told her.

CHAPTER ELEVEN

THE darkness clothed them like black velvet. Holly stood immobile by the light switch, knowing that it was not too late to change her mind, but then she heard Luke behind her, felt his warm breath on her neck and realised that she had no resistance left.

He slowly turned her round to him, his shape becoming a pale blur before her as her eyes began to gradually accustom themselves to the gloom of the room. He imprisoned her face in the warm cradle of his hand and she held her breath in fearful longing as she waited for him to speak. And when he did, the last of her foolish dreams crumbled like dust around her.

'You owe me, Holly,' he told her grimly. 'You owe me this.'

Her heart jerked with a judder of pain, but at that moment she vowed that he would never know the hurt he had caused her. And all the hurt to come...

'In lieu of rent?' she questioned smartly.

His mouth hardened. 'No.'

'Or for decorating the shop so nicely, perhaps?'

He laughed, but it was the bitterest laugh she had ever heard. 'Trying to shock me into leaving, are you? Well, it won't work, sweetheart. You decided to play this game, Holly—but maybe the stakes were higher than you imagined.'

'Luke—'

'No,' he whispered against her ear, and that deep velvet voice tugged relentlessly at her heartstrings even as she tried to steel herself against his words. 'You told Caroline what you pretty damned well pleased. You led her to believe we'd slept together and now she's gone. Well, you can't play God with people's lives and expect to get away with it. So now it's time to pay your dues, Holly, and I've come to collect.'

As he spoke he began to caress her, his hand moving expertly down the side of her body, sculpting the curves there as though he were fashioning her from damp clay, and Holly felt a shiver of longing ripple over her skin as despair sharpened her hunger instead of blunting it. She had waited her whole life to feel this kind of response to a man—so why in God's name did that man have to be Luke Goodwin?

All those books she had read, the paintings she had seen, every statue and film depicting the supposedly mindless passion which accompanied the act of love— hadn't she sometimes wondered whether it was a conspiracy and it was a figment of everyone's imagination?

But now she had discovered the power of desire for herself, and Luke was bringing it to life in her. Breathing passion and fire into her blood with his touch, until it blazed from every pore. 'Oh, Luke,' she sighed brokenly, as his fingers brushed negligently over the swell of her breasts. *'Oh!'*

'Come over here,' he said softly, taking her hand and leading her towards the back of the shop.

She couldn't bear to resist him. At that moment if he told her to walk naked into the street she honestly thought she might give it serious consideration. 'W-where?'

'Here.'

Here? Oh, my God, he was taking her into one of the changing rooms, where a bolt of silk dupion lay stacked on one side, like a giant ivory cylinder. The light was dim, but she saw his eyes glitter at the sight of the material, and he tugged at one end of the bolt, rolling it out so that it covered the entire floor of the cubicle in a great creamy, silken carpet. 'A bed for my beauty,' he mocked.

Holly's heart was thundering, her mouth so dry with excitement that she could barely articulate a word, let alone a sentence. 'We c-could always go upstairs?'

He swept a slow, possessive hand through the unruly tumble of her hair. 'I know we could,' he agreed softly. 'But I don't want to. Upstairs is yours, but this is no one's. I want to take you here, on this sumptuous covering in this anonymous room where no one has ever made love before, nor ever shall again. I want to see the apricot tones of your soft skin contrasted against the pale sheen of silk. I want to finish what I should have finished earlier…'

He began to swiftly unbutton her burgundy velvet bodice, and, even as her heart pulsed beneath his touch, she forced herself to close her mind to the matter-of-fact cruelty of his words—and of one word in particular.

Finish.

He wanted to finish what he had started earlier. He made her sound like an itch he needed to scratch.

She would have this one glorious initiation and then it would be over. Logic told her that she was crazy, that if she walked out now he would not force himself on her, nor beg. But her senses overrode all logic. She could not refuse him, nor would refuse him. She had dreamed too long of this moment to deny it now. Her body trembled as he discarded the waistcoat and turned his attention next to her white chiffon shirt.

His face was shadowed but the tension showed in the tight set of his jaw as he surveyed the dark-tipped globes which thrust towards him through the pale, gauzy material. 'Oh, God, yes,' he breathed, like a man bewitched. *'Yes.'*

Her breathing was shallow, and rapid as a hunted animal's, and yet he had scarcely touched her. Her cheeks were burning as she stood before him like a willing victim, not knowing what to do or what to say next.

Luke frowned. This was not how he had imagined it. He wanted fire from her, not fear. He wanted her to fight him, not accept him. This would be a glorious battle before it became a victory. 'Take your shirt off,' he told her unsteadily. 'Do it very, very *slowly*...'

Holly let out a long, low sigh. So this was what he wanted, was it? This was what would turn him on. And if he wanted her to play the vamp—then vamp she would be.

She lifted her chin proudly, feeling the heavy sway of curls falling down her back, then unhurriedly let one finger slowly circle the button of her shirt, as though the button itself were an erogenous zone. She heard him suck in a breath as she popped it open, and then another, another...until her breasts sprang free and then, to her surprise, he leaned forward to bury his head in them, holding her tightly by the waist for a moment, before letting his tongue and his lips taste each heavy and sensitive mound.

'Oh!' gasped Holly, her head falling back helplessly, her hands blindly seeking the thick, gold-tipped hair to balance herself as she swayed, saturated with desire, feeling his tongue wet and warm against her nipple.

'Is that good?' he demanded thickly.

It was heaven. She made an indistinct sound of assent as his teeth lightly scraped against the rosy tips which puckered and strained for his lips.

He fell to his knees before her, but she soon realised that it was no gesture of homage, merely a way that he could unbutton her velvet skirt with a speedy accuracy which spoke of lots of practice. It pooled with a whisper to the floor around her ankles, so that she was left wearing nothing but the unbuttoned chiffon shirt, minuscule white panties and a pair of knee-high black leather boots.

'My God!' he groaned. 'Holly!'

Vamps were verbal. 'What is it?' she whispered provocatively.

'This is like every fantasy I've ever had, condensed into one!' he groaned.

Vamps incited too. 'Just you wait,' she promised, wildly wondering whether she would be able to follow through.

'Lie down,' he urged her. 'Lie down just like that.'

She knew what to do. She lay on her back on the ivory satin, with her hands pillowed behind her head, her knees bent, and looked straight up into his face. Even through the gloom she could sense the sexual promise in the searing glance which he sent jackknifing through her.

Her heart pounded as she watched him drop his suit jacket to the floor, his hands unsteadily beginning to unbutton his shirt. Oh, God—she needed something to distract her from the moment of truth when Luke Goodwin would stand before her proud and naked.

'W-what do you want me to do?' she murmured, through lips which felt bee-stung swollen.

He stilled momentarily, and she saw the sudden twisting of his mouth. 'Straight sex bore you, does it?' he drawled, and she was certain that she could sense *disappointment* in his voice. Or was it contempt? He stood looking over her, and for one mad, terrible moment she thought he was about to change his mind and walk out.

But he didn't.

'Play with your breasts, baby,' he breathed shakily. 'Touch them, Holly. Pretend they're *my* hands. Go on...touch them.'

She had seen a dirty movie once. Someone at college had smuggled it into the film club for a joke, and Holly and three others had left halfway through. But she remembered how the buxom women had performed. The way they'd writhed their hips in exaggerated circles, moaning as they palpated their huge breasts as if they were kneading dough. And that was presumably what turned men on. Even so, she couldn't look him in the face as she did it.

She closed her eyes and began to run her hands experimentally over herself. It felt strange and wicked and oddly good, though nothing like as good as when *his* hands had been upon her. She risked raising her eyelashes by a centimetre, and through the shade of her lashes she could see Luke ripping his tie off and hurling it to the floor.

Next she heard the rasp of a zip and saw a grim look of determination on his face as he struggled to free himself—kicking first his trousers off and then his boxer shorts. And then...

Holly swallowed and screwed her eyes tightly shut. The only adult males she had ever seen in the nude before had been in a life class, and they hadn't been... hadn't been...

Dear Lord, she thought as she allowed her lashes to flutter up by a fraction, and fear skittered over her skin. If that was masculine arousal, then it was pretty daunting.

'Are you peeping, Holly?' he questioned silkily. 'Don't peep, sweetheart—open your eyes properly and take a good look at me.'

Running a nervous tongue over parchment lips, she did as he suggested.

'What's the matter?' he whispered. 'Afraid that this—' and he touched himself with a total, almost arrogant lack of self-consciousness '—will prove too much for you, Holly? Don't think you can take it?' He reached out his hand and without warning skimmed his finger down over the centre of her panties, wet with wanting now, the way they had never been before. She shuddered with pleasure as his finger came away moist from the cotton, and as he slowly licked the tip of it he gave a smile of desire and satisfaction.

'Oh, I think you can take me, Holly. You're so ripe and ready for me, sweetheart, and I haven't even started.'

He dropped to the ground over her, his knees to either side of her hips so that she was confronted with the sight of his manhood pushing a hard, tight column against his belly, and she gave a little moan of wonder. Forgetting everything, she raised her hand falteringly, then let it fall, but he captured it with his, raised it to his mouth and kissed it, his eyes never leaving her face.

'If you want to touch me, sweetheart—then I'm all yours.'

Curiosity made her reach out, her fingertips lightly skating down the broad, silken shaft.

He bore it for no more than a few seconds before his hand came down again, but this time it halted hers with steely insistence. 'Don't,' he said tersely.

'You don't like it?'

'You know damned well I do,' he ground out painfully, as he sucked in a deep breath of control.

'Then why stop?'

'No games, Holly.' His laugh was hollow. 'No games—okay? No pretence. This is going to be so good. *So* good. We both know that. Because you want me, baby—you want me real bad.'

What she had wanted was for him to kiss her. She wanted him to kiss her now. Oh, she wanted this, too—but a kiss was what she longed for.

And maybe he sensed it, for he lowered his head to hers. But the kiss was not sweet, or tender—it did nothing for her emotions but everything for her senses, making desire accelerate so rapidly that she felt she was spinning in a dark vortex where Luke was the only thing that mattered. He kissed her until she had no breath left in her body and every last trace of resistance had flown. With that kiss he claimed her and made her his.

Eventually he wonderingly raised his head, and carefully brushed a lock of hair from her face. 'Are you on the pill?'

She shook her head and began to blush, thanking heaven that the darkness meant he wouldn't be able to see. For heaven's sake, she had been touching him just about as intimately as a woman *could* touch a man—so why was the mention of contraception making her suddenly go all coy? Was she hurt that his words had been so prosaic, lacking the tenderness she had been longing to hear?

He took a condom from his pocket and slid it on, then moved back over her again, taking some of his weight on his elbows, and she shivered with anticipation as she felt the hard, warm weight of him. The feel of crisp, hair-roughened skin. Experimentally, she scraped her fingernails over the rock-hard globes of his buttocks, and felt him jerk beneath her touch with pleasure.

Luke looked down at her, revelling in the feel of her softness beneath him. He had longed for this moment since he had first seen her standing in all her colt-like beauty outside the shop, her face framed by the flames of her hair. She had been a fever in his blood ever since, and he wondered if only this would cure him of his obsession.

He trickled a leisurely finger over her peaking nipple, then bent and took the rosy nub into the warm, moist cavern of his mouth.

'Oh!' Holly's eyes shivered to a close as she felt his tongue slicking against her.

She felt his hand on the flat of her belly, circling its palm over the heat which radiated from her skin, and she felt her hips rise up to meet his, demanding more, *more*—as if instinct was controlling her and she no longer had dominance over her own body. She tried to pull his hand down to where the ache was becoming unbearable, but he wouldn't let her.

He laughed unsteadily. '*Yes!* You're greedy, Holly,' he whispered against her ear. 'I knew you would be. Wild, artistic, temperamental—seeking out every new sensation you can, is that it?'

Blindly she nodded her head, not knowing what she was agreeing to, only that if he didn't do something soon to ease this terrible wanting she would explode.

'Please, Luke...' she beseeched him. 'Oh, please!'

At *last*! This was where he had wanted her, soft and naked and writhing beneath him, begging him to bring her to fulfilment. That in itself should have been victory enough, and yet Luke was suddenly aware of a void...of this not being enough.

'Please,' she pleaded again.

His mouth hardened as he felt her impatience. She wanted satisfaction, and she wanted it quickly. 'You heartless little bitch,' he whispered, the sight of her naked against the luxurious folds of creamy silk exciting him to fever-pitch. 'I'm just a body to you, aren't I, Holly? A hot, slick machine designed to bring you pleasure.' But he drew in a deep breath until he had himself under control once more.

'W-what?' she stumbled, trying in vain to surface from this enchantment.

'Nothing.' He let his hand drift downwards, a featherlight flick to where she was taut and molten, and she gasped. 'God, you're responsive,' he murmured, disbelief growing on his face as he realised how close to the edge she was. He flicked again, then circled, around and around, and felt her arch beneath him, her body stretched with unbearable tightness until the spasms began and he could feel her pulsing beneath his finger, while she clung to him, making little cries of pleasure into his ear.

Her eyes flickered open as the sensations began to fade, and she looked at him in bewilderment. 'W-what happened?'

'What *happened*? You had just about the quickest orgasm on record, sweetheart, that's what happened.'

She gave him a befuddled gaze. 'But I…I don't understand.'

His laugh was as cold as his body was hot and longing to thrust into her moist heat. 'Oh, come on—baby—I think we're both a little too experienced to fall for that one, don't you? Though it's a pretty good line to take, I give you that.'

She stared up at him in confusion, as if he were speaking to her in a foreign language. 'Line? What line?'

'Do you imply that to all your lovers?' he whispered. 'That you've never had an orgasm before? Does it flatter them? Swell their egos—and maybe something else, besides?' He gave a throaty laugh. 'Well, there's no need to invent things on my account, Holly, and I certainly don't need any encouragement to incite me. Feel for yourself.' And he took her hand, guided it to him, folded her fingers around the great throbbing width of him.

'Luke,' she said again, only this time it was halfway between a gasp and a sob.

'I want to savour this,' he murmured, as he began to position himself above her. 'Every sweet moment. Every stroke I make and every cry you utter. I'm going to imprint myself on your soul, my angel, give you so much pleasure that you will recoil in disgust if any other man ever tries to touch you.'

But for all his brutal words, he experienced a sense of wonder as he thrust deeply into her, and Holly felt a swift, piercing spasm before her muscles clenched and then exquisitely unclenched to accommodate him.

'God, you're so tight,' he whispered, and kissed her. Tighter than he'd ever known. Or was it simply that he was more excited than he had ever been in his life? He found that he was trembling, that he could hardly bear to stop kissing her. He began to move slowly inside her. 'I'm going to make you come again,' he promised. 'Would you like that?'

Mutely, she nodded, and hooked her hand around his neck, bringing his head down to hers and opening her mouth to his. This time the kiss was sweet, but perhaps it was made all the sweeter by the communion of flesh, those great strokes which filled her, heated her, sent her hurtling towards that place again.

His resolve was steely until he felt her nearing the brink, and only then did he allow himself to relax into it. He had never been harder or fuller or closer, but he kept drawing back and drawing back, until he felt her suck in a great breath, waited until she had started to shudder beneath him, and only then did he let go, his last fleeting thought being that it had never been as good as this before. Never. His grip on her tightened. 'Love me, Holly,' he breathed shakily. 'Oh, love me!' And his universe dissolved.

As consciousness returned, so did sensation. Holly became aware of the silky fabric which lay rucked up beneath her naked flesh, and of the wetness between her legs.

Luke felt it, too, and raised his head. 'I think the condom may have burst,' he told her ruefully, realising that, stupidly, he didn't care. He kissed her bare shoulder and slid his hand down between her legs, but his fingers came away oddly sticky...

He rolled off her and snapped on the cubicle light, then stared down in disbelief at the tell-tale scarlet stain which had flowered over the creamy silk, his eyes widening with horror as he realised the full implications.

'Blood,' he breathed. *'Blood.'* He turned to her with disbelief written in his eyes, and, before he could hide it, pride. A primitive, unimaginable pride. 'Holly. Holly, sweetheart—you're a...'

But the tender words had come too late. 'Yes, I'm a virgin!' she spat back at him. 'Surprised?'

'Surprised? I'm absolutely bloody flabbergasted,' he admitted in a dazed voice, until he realised from the look on her face that it was entirely the *wrong* thing to say. 'Holly, sweetheart—come here—'

'Get *away* from me!' she told him furiously, and she pushed him away and jumped to her feet. He snaked his hand out and tried to capture her ankle, but she shook him off, hurriedly pulled her shirt back on and then wiped the thin scarlet film of blood from her thighs with her discarded panties.

'Holly—'

'Don't you "Holly" me!' she declared furiously, and pointed at the stained fabric. 'Why don't you take the evidence of my virginity and wave it triumphantly out of the window?' she raged. 'That's what they used to do in the barbaric old days, isn't it? Well—that should suit you right down to the ground!'

'Listen to me—'

'I won't listen to another word you say, Luke Goodwin! And you can take your smug, outdated hypocrisy somewhere else! How *dare* you think you can suddenly elevate me from tramp to Madonna—just because I happened to have an intact hymen!' She drew in a deep, shuddering breath, but not before she had seen his shocked expression. *Good!* Then she'd shock him some more! 'We've both had what we want, so now you can go! I'm sorry I lied to your fiancée about sleeping with you—but, if you want to know the truth, at the time I thought she wasn't good enough for you. Now I think you're probably a match made in heaven! It may not be too late, Luke—so why don't you go crawling back to Africa and find her?'

'I'm not going anywhere until we've talked this over sensibly. I've told you—it's over with Caroline. She's gone back.'

But his words brought her no joy. 'And I told you that I don't *care*—and nothing will ever change that fact!'

He should have looked ridiculous, sitting naked among the sheening undulations of the ruffled silk, but, oddly enough, he looked divine. 'Holly.' His voice was soft. 'Not to talk about this is crazy.'

Holly closed her heart and glowered. 'It's too *late*!

There's nothing left to say. I've paid my *dues*,' she told him deliberately, and saw him flinch. 'So get out. Out of my shop and out of my life! And don't come back! I *mean* it, Luke!'

He could see she did. He could also see that nothing he said right now would help. If he tried to gentle her, then he would be accused of patronising her. If he tried to love her he would be the sex-crazed taker of her innocence. This might be the hardest thing he had ever had to do, but…

Rising to his feet, Luke began to reach down for his clothes while Holly, with folded arms and trembling lips, stood and watched him.

She meant every word she'd said, but that didn't stop her from having to bite back bitter tears as he silently began to pull on his trousers, ready to leave her.

CHAPTER TWELVE

THE mammoth Christmas tree twinkled merrily in the sumptuous dining room of the Grantchester hotel, and Holly pushed her barely touched plate of lobster away.

'Have another glass of champagne, darling!'

'I don't want another glass of champagne, thank you,' answered Holly moodily, slapping her hand over the crystal flute before her mother could tip any more wine into it.

'It might put you in a better mood,' said her mother carefully. She'd never known her compliant Holly be so grumpy!

'It might also give me a splitting headache,' objected Holly. 'And I've got to drive back to Woodhampton.'

'Darling, *not* tonight—it's New Year's Eve,' protested her mother, although not, Holly noticed, terribly convincingly.

But who could blame her?

Since Holly had arrived to spend Christmas with her mother and husband number four at one of London's most luxurious hotels, she was aware that she had been like a bear with a sore head. Oh, she had gone through all the motions of seasonal celebration, but she knew that she hadn't put up a very convincing performance.

Her mother lit a cigarette. 'Are you going to a New Year party, then, darling?'

Holly shook her head, and flapped her hand to dispel

some of the fog. 'Nope. But I promised that the draw for the wedding dress would take place on the stroke of midnight!'

'Huh!' scoffed her mother. 'Who's going to be there to see it? Who will know if you draw it tomorrow morning instead? That way you can stay on and party here, with us!'

'*I'll* know,' said Holly firmly. 'And besides, I don't want to spoil your fun, Mum,' she added truthfully.

Holly's mother looked guilty as she refilled her glass. 'Darling, I know I haven't been a good mother—'

Holly sighed. It was getting to that melancholy stage of the lunch. 'You did your best, Mum,' she said placatingly. 'That's all anyone can do. You're you, and I'm me.' She sniffed miserably. 'And I just happened to make the mistake of falling in love with the biggest rat this side of the Atlantic!'

'This is this *Luke*, is it? The man you won't tell me anything about other than his name and the fact that he might be a member of the rodent family?'

'That's right,' said Holly, staring gloomily into her empty glass.

'It is rather irritating, darling,' objected her mother prettily. 'You've never shown interest in a single man in your *life*, and now you have done and you won't tell me anything about him!'

'That's because there's nothing to tell, other than he's left and probably gone back to Africa! He's past tense!' she snarled. 'History!'

Her mother lifted her shoulders expressively. '*Men,*' she colluded darkly. 'They're all the same!' She batted her eyelashes as she saw the squat, toad-like shape of husband number four approaching across the restaurant, and hissed, 'But they keep you in comfort as you get older, dear! Just remember that!'

Holly shuddered as she rose to her feet. She would rather stay single, thank you very much, than rely on some odious creep to support her!

Half an hour later, she was driving fast out of London towards Woodhampton in her Beetle. The garage that Luke had recommended had telephoned to renew their offer, and it seemed like an indecent amount of money for the gaudy car. 'Beetles are *big* right now!' the salesman had informed her.

But while the sensible side of her urged her to take the money and run…well, there was another side which couldn't bear to part with the car. God knew, she hadn't got Luke—was she going to lose everything else that was dear to her?

All the way back, her thoughts threatened to drive her crazy. However brutish Luke had been, the unchangeable fact was that she missed him more each day, and the longer he was out of her life, the greater the temptation to justify his behaviour.

All right, he hadn't told her about Caroline—but his behaviour had been exemplary while she'd been staying with him. Yes, they had been close—but their closeness had been no more sinister than warmth and affection. He hadn't laid a finger on her in the whole two weeks, and that must have taken some self-control since she had spent the entire time giving him the green light.

And afterwards, in her flat after the party—he hadn't exactly been guilty of a capital crime *there* either, had he? What had he done? Touched her ankle and *kissed* her. Big deal! It had been a *party*, for heaven's sake, and, like her mother said, people always kissed people they shouldn't at parties. Why, it was how her mother had found most of her boyfriends and all of her husbands!

Woodhampton High Street was deserted, but loud disco music was blaring from the fairy-lit interior of the Bell Inn, and Holly remembered that they were having a New Year party. She thought she'd probably pass on that…

She parked outside Lovelace Brides and couldn't resist turning her head to look up at Apson House, hope flickering in her heart despite all her best attempts to stem it. But the house was in complete darkness, with not a flicker of light anywhere to be seen.

So he wasn't back and he obviously had no intention of coming back. He had missed Africa and had probably managed to change Caroline's mind, and no doubt they were busy planning a romantic, open-air wedding out there right now.

She fished around in her bag for her keys, her eyes automatically flickering to the window, where the prize dress was spotlit, then back to her handbag again.

She stilled.

Narrowing her eyes, she turned and looked back towards the window. Everything looked exactly the same as when she had left it, and yet it was *not* the same.

For it was *her* dress in the window, and yet it was *not* her dress.

Fingers shaking, she managed to get the door open, and stepped into the half-light of the interior, where the spotlight focussed so brightly on the wedding dress gave out the only illumination.

Holly walked forward, slowly as a sleepwalker, until she was just feet away from the gown, and then her hands began to tremble. She reached forward to touch it, and the difference became evident in a moment. Her mother's gown was made of far costlier material than hers, the stitching on it exquisitely fine. Holly's wedding gown was a beautiful dress, but her mother's was an heirloom.

'Like it?' came a deep voice from the shadows.

It should have given her a fright, but it didn't—it was a voice she had grown to love and which she recognised immediately. She didn't even turn round, but then maybe that was because she could sense he was moving across the shop towards her, and she didn't speak until he was right behind her.

'Where did you find it?' she asked dully.

'Long story.'

She did turn round then, and she could do absolutely nothing to stop the great rush of emotion which washed over her. She'd missed him, she realised, more than she had any right to miss him.

She met his gaze. 'No need to ask how you got in.'

He shrugged. 'The landlord always has a spare key.' He looked at her face closely for some kind of reaction. 'Surprised to see me?'

She thought about it. 'I'm not sure.'

He thought that her voice contained neither warmth, nor chill—just a matter-of-factness which was oddly emotionless. She sounded like a tired teacher at the end of term.

She frowned. 'Have you lost weight?'

'Yeah.' His voice was wry. 'Haven't had a lot of appetite recently.'

Me neither, she thought, but, 'Oh,' was all she said. She wanted to ask what *his* reason was, but that might sound as if she was concerned about his welfare, and she wasn't. Because she still hadn't forgiven him.

He threw her a conciliatory look. 'Do you want to know about the dress?'

She wasn't going to make this easy for him. 'I'd rather know the truth about you and Caroline.'

He nodded. 'I thought you might say something like that. Can we go and sit down somewhere more comfortable while I tell you?'

'Where did you have in mind?' she asked nastily. 'The changing room?'

Luke resisted the temptation to say, If you like, and shook his tawny head instead. 'Upstairs?'

'I thought you didn't like my flat!' she snapped.

He had come prepared for a fight, but even so it was the hardest thing in the world to just tiptoe round her raw feelings like this, when all he wanted to do was to scoop her up in his arms and kiss the breath out of her.

'I like your flat very much, Holly,' he told her equably. 'But if you'd prefer we could talk somewhere else. How about the quiet, intimate atmosphere of The Bell?'

Her mouth began to twitch, but she wouldn't laugh, she *wouldn't*. 'Come on, then,' she said ungraciously, and stomped loudly up the stairs, like a child sent early to bed, while he followed her.

The flat was warm. 'Have you turned the heating on?' she demanded suspiciously.

'Guilty.'

'But why? I might not have been back at least until the day after tomorrow. The shop won't open on New Year's Day.'

'I know. But I also knew that you'd be back to-night—'

'How could you know *that*, for heaven's sake?'

'Because that's when you said the draw would take place.'

Holly nodded, pleased that he had remembered and pleased that he had taken her at her word. But if he had *really* taken her at her word, then he wouldn't be here, would he? Not when she had told him that she never wanted to see him again.

She sat down on the sofa and looked at him, steeling herself against the denim-blue eyes, the tawny head, the irresistible mouth.

'I guess it would be an unfair advantage of me to sit down beside you?'

'Yes, it would—and it's a little late in the day for old-fashioned courtesy,' she scolded, despairing of herself as she added, 'You can sit right up at the other end as long as you don't move.'

He did, stretching his long legs out in front of him before turning to look at her. 'And I guess you want an explanation of my behaviour?'

'Damn right I do!'

His eyes narrowed. 'And then perhaps you'll explain to me why you let me take your virginity in the most inglorious fashion imaginable?'

'Because I ''owed'' you?' she mocked.

He winced. 'You know that I would never have said that if I'd had any idea that—'

'That I wasn't the strumpet you had me down as?'

Luke sighed. 'Sweetheart, you are an enigmatic woman.' His mouth softened as he tried to put it into words. 'There's just something about you. You have the kind of eyes…the kind of lips…a certain way of looking…'

'Just what exactly are you trying to say, Luke?'

'That you look like someone who's been around the block several times over!' Seeing her perplexed look, he elaborated. 'It didn't occur to me that you weren't sexually experienced!'

'Because I'm twenty-six?'

'No.' He shook his head. 'It's nothing to do with your age. Just the way you looked at me the first time you met me—well…' he shrugged '…without wishing to sound arrogant—'

'Oh, cut the false modesty, Luke, *please!*'

'You looked like you just wanted me to drag you off to the nearest bed and ravish you all night long.'

'It's a look you recognise well, is it?' she asked sarcastically.

'Well, women *have* come on to me like that before,' he admitted.

'And you always take them up on it, I suppose?'

'Well, no—I don't! That's the whole point!'

'What, never?' she queried, in disbelief.

'Not for years, no. Not that instant wham-bam-thank-you-ma'am thing, anyway.'

'That must be some small comfort for Caroline.

Remember Caroline, Luke? The fiancée whom you conveniently forgot to mention?'

'I was coming to that.'

'I can't imagine that there's anything you could tell me about Caroline which would make your behaviour forgivable.'

'Are you going to let me try?'

She shrugged, knowing she was going to say yes and feeling weak because of it—but how could she get through the rest of her life not knowing the truth? 'I suppose so.'

He stared at his hands, at the jagged scar down the side of one thumb. He'd nearly lost the digit, and remembered the pain he had felt at the time—but that was nothing compared to the agonising ache inside him now. 'I've known Caroline for a long time,' he began. 'Years and years. She was a teacher at the nearest school to my ranch and we used to meet at various socials.'

'How nice for you both! Was it love at first sight?'

'Not at all. She used to heartily disapprove of my lifestyle and I never thought of her in that way. I used to look on her as a friend.'

'So what happened to change her mind? Your undoubted prowess in bed—or maybe I should say on bolts of pure silk?'

At least he had saved his trump card for exactly this moment; he just prayed that he hadn't destroyed all her faith in him, because if he had she would never believe him... He drew a deep breath. 'Actually, I've never slept with Caroline. Never.'

'You've never slept with me either,' she put in pointedly.

It was not the reaction he had wanted—it sounded so unforgiving, and it started him thinking about things he hadn't planned to think about. Not yet...

Sexual tension crackled through the air as their gazes locked with erotic memories. 'Okay—let me phrase that a little differently. I've never had sex with Caroline,' he told her baldly. 'Ever.'

She stared at the wall unseeingly. 'I'm not sure that I believe you.'

'Yes, I thought you'd say that. But it's true, Holly. I haven't.'

Hope stirred with a flicker in her heart, but she kept every trace of it from her voice. 'Why not?'

He hesitated. He had never been disloyal to a woman in his life, and he certainly wasn't going to start being disloyal to Caroline now, but these past weeks he had been left wondering whether some minor brainstorm might have afflicted him this past year. 'Because she thought that not having sex until we'd made some kind of commitment would make me respect her more. That's how some women think.'

Oh, God—so what did that say about *her*?

'Holly, let me try to explain to you. Do you want me to?'

A small voice. 'Yes.'

He forced himself to concentrate on the past; it was the only way he could stop himself from taking her into his arms and just holding her until all the hurt had left her beautiful face. 'I once told you that my life has been chequered. That I've been rootless and wandering for a long time, and working on a game reserve allowed me to carry on living that life legitimately. A kind of paid-up nomad. Do you understand?'

She nodded. 'I think so.'

'Until earlier this year, when I looked around at what I had, and it just didn't seem enough any more—'

'You mean, money-wise?'

He shook his head. 'No, not money-wise. I'm talking fundamentals. I asked myself did I want to still be doing what I was doing when I was sixty, and the answer was a very loud no.'

'And then you inherited?'

'Then I inherited,' he echoed. 'And my relationship with Caroline changed.' He saw the way she pursed her lips. 'Oh, I know what you're thinking, and I agree— that Caroline would never have agreed to marry if I hadn't inherited. I knew that.'

'You *knew* that?' she asked, outraged. 'That she was a gold-digger?'

He smiled at the old-fashioned term. 'Life isn't as simple as that, Holly. Caroline wouldn't have been interested in marrying a ranch manager who slept out under the stars. She wanted stability and she *offered* stability, and for a while there I thought that's what I wanted, too. And my inheritance gave *me* the stability that I'd been lacking up until then.

'We talked of marriage—I *didn't* propose, and I bought her no ring—we talked of marriage in an abstract way. The way people used to talk about marriage—as an institutional framework in which to bring up children, and I certainly didn't want to miss out on having children. Neither did she.

'But there was no romantic love—that's one of the

reasons I convinced myself it might work. No great passion—but we got along together pretty well. Nothing was definite, but I had to come over to sort out my uncle's affairs, and we decided to use that space to think it over. To decide whether that was what we both really wanted.'

'And Caroline certainly decided that the answer was "yes", didn't she?' demanded Holly.

'Yes, she did. But I had done exactly the opposite. I had started to feel uneasy about the cold-bloodedness of such an arrangement. And I had seen you and it was like a thunderbolt that knocked me right off balance. I fought it because I thought it was simply romantic love, a love which would fade.' He sighed.

'And then you came to stay with me, and I realised that it wasn't going to fade. That this was it. Love. The real thing—and all-consuming. The only thing that mattered any more. I'd denied it and fought it all my life, but now it had finally happened—and how!'

She looked at him in confusion. 'But why? Why fight it?'

'Because I was pretty short on female role models when I was growing up, Holly,' he told her urgently, and it was as though he had lifted a veil from before her eyes. 'There were none at boarding-school, unless you counted the matron, and no one did. My mother was the only one I had, and she died before I had time to get to know the real woman she was, because as a child your perception is distorted by dependence.

'And after she died, I saw her through my father's eyes—as feckless and beautiful. Because he was besotted with her and yet he resented feeling that way. She made a fool of him over and over again, and yet he never stopped loving her. And I was determined that the same fate would never befall me.' He saw the slope of her shoulders relax, and began to let himself cling onto a grain of hope.

'You had the same kind of bewitching beauty as she did, and it terrified me. It terrified me enough to realise that I couldn't possibly marry Caroline, not when I felt that way about someone else. So I flew back to Africa, to tell her.'

So *that* was where he had gone! 'Only she wasn't there,' she realised wonderingly. 'Caroline had unexpectedly brought herself over here and was busy choosing a surprise wedding dress.'

'I came back to fireworks. When I found out you'd let Caroline believe we'd slept together, I was almost *exultant*—'

'*Exultant?*'

'Of course.' He shrugged. 'It meant that I could now cast you in the role of the bad fairy—allowing me to keep my prejudices alive. It meant that I could have you...' his mouth curved into a sexy line '...in the truest sense of the word—and afterwards I would be free of my obsession for you.'

'But it didn't work like that?'

He shook his head. 'No, it didn't—not with you, sweetheart. You had ensnared and captivated me, and then I made the most catastrophic discovery of all—that you were completely innocent. It blew my mind—'

'I thought you liked that,' she argued, as she remembered that almost *smug* look of pride which had darkened his features.

He gave a slow smile. 'Well, of course I *liked* it—'

'But?'

'It wasn't a question of not *liking* it, just that I felt so bad about my attitude towards you. I would have been more gentle if I'd known. More loving…much more loving.' He looked at her properly then, a question burning in the dazzling blue fire of his eyes. 'Why was I the first?' he asked her bluntly. 'Did someone put you off men, sweetheart? Are you hiding some kind of heartbreak?'

She shook her head. 'No heartbreak, no. In fact, there was nothing before you. Nothing at all, not in the way of feelings. I'd never been in love before, and sex without love just wasn't an option for me.' She sighed. 'You see, we're all victims of circumstance to some extent, Luke—and I had grown up seeing my mother use men. I saw relationships as a bartering mechanism—sex for money, if we're being honest.' And they *were* being honest, she realised, both of them, more honest than she'd ever been before. But how honest dared she be?

'Tell me,' he urged, and she heard vulnerability there, and realised in that moment that this big, strong, adventuring man needed her reassurance just as much as she needed his.

'I never felt for anyone the love I felt for you,' she said simply.

'Felt?'

She smiled. 'Feel. Present tense. And future tense.'

'Future perfect tense?' He grinned as he took hold of her hand and pulled her towards him. 'Please come here right now, because I think I'll die if I don't kiss you soon.'

'Oh, Luke,' she sighed dreamily, and went straight into his arms.

His features softened. 'Now look at me and listen, Holly Lovelace,' he said sternly. 'I love you—'

'Luke—'

'And I was wrong to think that I could make reality go away by pretending it didn't exist. I should have done things differently, but, oh, sweetheart—I guess that deep down I didn't want to run the risk of losing you.'

She nodded, remembering that she had been his for the taking at Apson House. But he hadn't taken. 'And Caroline?' she asked slowly.

'Is justifiably furious, but not heartbroken—'

'She must be! *I* would be!'

'She wasn't in love with me, Holly,' he said gently. 'Not ever. It was a transaction of the head, not the heart—and I'm not just saying that to make you, or me, feel better. It's true.' He hesitated. 'Caroline craves security over everything else, it's the one thing she hasn't got—'

'She hasn't got you any more.'

'But I was never hers to have, not really.' He looked into her eyes and she read so many things in his. Love. Regret. Hope. Trust.

'Would you mind if I bought her a house?' he asked softly.

'Of course I don't mind.' Holly traced the outline of his lips with her finger. 'Do you think she'll accept it?'

'I'll ask her—she can only say no.'

Holly couldn't imagine anyone saying no to Luke, but then he started kissing her, and it wasn't until some time later that she got a chance to ask, 'So how did you find my mother's dress?'

'It wasn't easy,' he admitted. 'But I was determined to do it.' His eyes had never looked bluer as they read the question in hers. 'As some kind of peace-offering, I guess, because I felt so bad about everything. After you kicked me out, I went back to the house to change, and I started thinking about Ursula—'

Holly blinked. He certainly was a man of surprises. 'Why?'

'I wondered if maybe she knew more about your mother's dress than she realised.' He swept a hand back through the thick, gold-tipped hair. 'I knew she was staying at The Bell that night, so I went to see her and found out which local newspaper *her* mother had advertised the dress in. Luckily it still existed. So then I travelled down to London to see the editor.'

'What on earth for?'

'Well, I thought it would make a good Christmas story. To find out if the person who had bought it still read that newspaper. The editor agreed to run a piece on it, to see what it would turn up.'

'And what happened?' asked Holly, fascinated now.

'The woman who bought it contacted me and told me the whole story. She had been let down. She bought the dress for a wedding which never took place—because the man she was in love with was married to someone else. He'd spun her the oldest story in the book and abandoned her when she was just a couple of weeks pregnant.'

'Oh, *no*,' said Holly, and bit down painfully on her lip.

'She grew to hate the dress, but she could never bear to get rid of it because it was so beautiful. Later, she thought about selling it once or twice, but no one offered her anywhere near its true worth.'

'So what did you do?' breathed Holly.

'I met with her and offered to buy the dress from her—'

'For a lot of money?'

'For what it would be worth today.'

Holly gave a low whistle. 'That's a hell of a lot of money.'

His eyes were very blue. 'Small compensation for the hurt she had suffered.'

'And she agreed?''

'She was delighted—her only proviso was that there should be no publicity, and I could understand that. So, I'm giving you back the dress, Holly.'

'And the catch?'

'No catch.' He shook his head. 'It's yours—to do what you want with.'

She looked down into her hands for a moment, and when she lifted her head again her green eyes were very bright. 'I think I'd quite like to wear it,' she told him softly. 'In church.'

Luke smiled. 'That's what I was hoping you'd say.'

Michelle McCormack was feeling flustered as she repositioned a dark green leaf. 'Holly, will you please hurry *up*?' she scolded. 'Everyone is there. The vicar is there. Luke is there. Much more time and I'm sure that some of your arty friends are going to kidnap him—I

overheard one girl say quite shamelessly that she'd love
to sculpt him!'

'I'll bet she did,' agreed Holly calmly. 'And she probably has no intention of using marble!'

'Holly!' Michelle's voice softened. 'You look wonderful. Just wonderful.'

'Do I?' Holly stared at herself in the mirror. It seemed
strange to be preparing for *her* wedding, in *her* shop.
She was the first bride to wear her mother's dress and it
looked perfect. 'It doesn't look dated at all, does it?'

'Not at all—and you're the most beautiful bride I've
ever seen,' said Michelle honestly.

'You look pretty nifty in that outrageous hat yourself!'

Holding Holly's bouquet, Michelle came up behind
her to look in the mirror, and the two of them silently
observed the stunning impact of the thick, ivory satin
and the delicate pleating at the waist. In Holly's hair was
a coronet of copper roses and dark, glossy green leaves
which echoed her bouquet.

Luke had chosen the flowers, much to Michelle's
amusement and envy. 'I've never met a man who chose
his bride's flowers before,' she sighed. 'But he insisted.
The roses were to match your hair, he said; the leaves
your eyes.'

'Shame they don't do any green flowers,' smiled
Holly serenely.

Michelle briefly switched from soft romantic mode to
frustrated florist. 'Well, as it's an Easter wedding, I was
hoping for something like lilies, or pansies—'

Holly's voice softened to a smoky whisper. 'But that's
traditional, and Luke's not traditional, Michelle—*you*
know that.'

'Luke's just gorgeous—beginning and end of story—and you're a very lucky woman.' Michelle shot her friend a glance. 'You are *okay*, aren't you, Holly?'

'Mmm?'

'I mean—you seem awfully *distracted*—you have done all week! You're not having any second thoughts, are you?'

Holly giggled as she shook her head, the copper curls contained today beneath the fragrant circlet of roses. 'Not a single one,' she said firmly. 'Why?'

Michelle frowned. 'You just seem *different*, that's all. There's a kind of *bloom* about you, and—' her brown eyes narrowed assessingly '—that dress looks a little small around the waistband—'

Holly burst out laughing. 'Why don't you just come right out and ask me?' she teased. 'It isn't a secret you know, not really.'

'You're *pregnant*?' breathed Michelle.

'Yes, I am.'

Michelle's eyes were like saucers. 'But what about your *shop*? What's going to happen to it?'

Holly shrugged her shoulders, a dreamy smile curving her lips. 'Oh, the shop no longer seems like my be-all and end-all. It was the freedom to design and make my own wedding dresses that I craved—and, fortunately, that fits in very nicely with motherhood. Luke says...' she sighed with pleasure '...that I can have someone in to run the shop if I want. Maybe even start a co-operative to help young, talented designers who don't have the good fortune to win competitions. Several of the girls I was at college with have already expressed a *huge* interest about coming to live here!'

'Surprising, that,' offered Michelle drily. 'Maybe they think they'll end up marrying millionaires, too!'

'Luke isn't a millionaire, not really,' said Holly firmly. 'Lots of his inheritance is in assets—'

'I know. It's a hard life!' teased Michelle. 'But you are a *lucky*, *lucky* woman, Holly Lovelace!'

'I'd have married him if he'd still been that man sleeping out under the stars,' said Holly truthfully.

'I know you would, dummy.' Michelle's voice was soft. 'I meant lucky that you're carrying his child.'

Holly turned, as pleased and surprised by the intimacy of the old-fashioned term as by her friend's response to her news. 'That's not the reaction you expect if the bride waddles down the aisle.'

Michelle looked at Holly's tall, slim figure and shook her head. '*Waddle?* Do me a favour, Holly—at twenty-eight weeks you'll probably have the same kind of figure that most of us have, and we're *not* pregnant!'

'Why lucky, then?' asked Holly curiously.

'Oh, because you've found Luke, and he's found you, and quite honestly it's restored my faith in men to see him look at you the way he does when he thinks no one is watching.' She sniffed, then glared. 'There I go again! Much more emotion and I'll start blubbing—and I can't afford to let my mascara run. Have you *seen* Luke's best man?'

'Well, of course I've seen him! His name's Will, and he's very nice.'

'I know,' sighed Michelle. 'He just wasn't what I expected. Terribly English, isn't he—in a way that Luke isn't?'

'They were at school together,' explained Holly. "I'll introduce you afterwards, if you like.'

'Mmm! Yes, *please*!' Michelle made a final adjustment to her outrageous hat. 'Oh, and my friend Mary said to wish you all the best, and to be sure and tell you that she's over the moon at winning the wedding dress.'

'Good. Should be perfect for a summer wedding.' Holly smiled with satisfaction. 'So everybody's happy.' She held out her hand for her bouquet. A moment's quiet reflection, and she felt ready.

'Come on, Michelle,' she said softly. 'Let's go.'

The organist was coping admirably with some African music which Luke had had sent over. It was livelier than the usual offering at an English country wedding, and already the congregation were getting into the swing of things. A couple of people had even been noticed swaying their shoulders!

Holly's mother had left husband number four sipping champagne cocktails back at the hotel. Men never really appreciated a wedding in the way that a woman did! He would only cramp her style, and she intended to bask in the reflected glory of the wedding dress that *she* had designed all those years ago. She sighed. If only she had known then what she knew now...

She sat next to Ursula O'Neil, who had been surprised and delighted to be invited to the wedding. But, as Holly had explained, if it hadn't been for Ursula, then she would never have got the dress back. Ursula's sister Amber had also been invited, but had declined. She had called her own wedding off at the last minute, and said she couldn't face seeing the inside of a church for the time being.

Caroline had been invited but, as expected, had declined. She had sent them six very ugly place-mats and explained that she would be far too busy furnishing her brand-new house to attend.

At the altar Luke sat next to Will, just enjoying the music and the sight of sunlight streaming cobalt, scarlet, jade and saffron through the stained glass windows. He felt...well, he felt just great. He would even go so far as to say that he was the happiest man on earth. He didn't know what the future held; no one did. Whether their baby would be born here, or in Africa. But Holly was flexible and so was he. Nothing seemed to matter any more, now that they had found one another.

The lively music stilled, and then began to play the traditional notes of the 'Wedding March', and Luke, together with the rest of the congregation, slowly rose to his feet.

He didn't know whether he was supposed to or not, but Holly was in the same building and therefore he just couldn't resist turning round to look at her.

She took the slow, careful steps of every bride—the pure, clear light from the windows turning the buttery satin of her dress into a soft kaleidoscope of colour. The understated beauty of the copper roses only emphasised her exquisite colouring. God, how he loved her.

Holly saw him watching her and smiled back, a look of pure happiness.

Luke's heart thundered as their gazes held for a private, infinitesimal moment, and he knew that everything was going to be just perfect.

He had come home at last.

HARLEQUIN PRESENTS®

WANTED: ONE WEDDING DRESS

A trilogy by

Sharon Kendrick

Three brides in search of the perfect dress—and the perfect husband!

In February 1999 wedding-dress designer
Holly Lovelace marries the man of her dreams in
One Bridegroom Required!
Harlequin Presents® #2011

In March 1999 Amber has her big day in
One Wedding Required!
Harlequin Presents® #2017

In April 1999 Ursula, Amber's sister,
walks up the aisle, too!
One Husband Required!
Harlequin Presents® #2023

Available wherever Harlequin books are sold.

HARLEQUIN®
*M*akes any time special ™

Coming Next Month

HARLEQUIN ◆ PRESENTS®

THE BEST HAS JUST GOTTEN BETTER!

#2013 CONTRACT BABY Lynne Graham
(The Husband Hunters)
Becoming a surrogate mother was Polly's only option when her mother needed a life-saving operation. But the baby's father was businessman Raul Zaforteza, and he would do anything to keep his unborn child—even marry Polly....

#2014 THE MARRIAGE SURRENDER Michelle Reid
(Presents Passion)
When Joanna had no choice but to turn to her estranged husband, Sandro, for help, he agreed, but on one condition: that she return to his bed—as his wife. But what would happen when he discovered her secret?

#2015 THE BRIDE WORE SCARLET Diana Hamilton
When Daniel Faber met his stepbrother's mistress, Annie Kincaid, he decided the only way he could keep her away from his stepbrother was to kidnap her! But the plan had a fatal flaw—Daniel had realized he wanted Annie for himself!

#2016 DANTE'S TWINS Catherine Spencer
(Expecting!)
it wasn't just jealous colleagues who believed Leila was marrying for money; so did her boss, and fiancé Dante Rossi! How could Leila marry him without convincing him she was more than just the mother of his twins?

#2017 ONE WEDDING REQUIRED! Sharon Kendrick
(Wanted: One Wedding Dress)
Amber was delighted to be preparing to marry her boss, hunky Finn Fitzgerald. But after she gave an ill-advised interview to an unscrupulous journalist, it seemed there wasn't going to be a wedding at all....

#2018 MISSION TO SEDUCE Sally Wentworth
Allie was certain she didn't need bodyguard Drake Marsden for her assignment in Russia. But Drake refused to leave her day or night, and then he decided that the safest place for her was in his bed!